A Pride & Prejudice
Time Travel Romance

THE MEMORY SERIES #1

NEY MITCH

ISBN: 978-1-68046-756-7

Published by Satin Romance
An Imprint of Melange Books, LLC
White Bear Lake, MN 55110
www.satinromance.com

Published in the United States of America.

Cover Design by Caroline Andrus

# Foreword

Reader, welcome to the Second Edition of 'Moments of Moments Past'. Thanks for trying a new read! Just a precaution, due to Elizabeth travelling in time, there shall be references to pop culture in modern day as she grows accustomed to our times and Mr. Darcy helps her along the way. To anyone who finds themselves willing to take up this novel and wishes to read a time travel tale where Mr. Darcy and Elizabeth Bennet meet in two different time periods, thanks for everything. I hope you enjoy!

# Prologue

I t's a tendency of humankind to believe in miracles, but then do not believe them when we see them.

If it were not for what I had undergone, I never would have thought this even possible, yet it was!

I suppose though, that when you eliminate the impossible, whatever remains, however improbable, must be the truth. I cannot pin that theory down to me, for it was written by a writer in the distant future named Arthur Doyle. He began to publish the series he used that quote for in 1888, which would be eight years after I was recorded to have passed away, at 94 years old.

A strange thing it is, to know what year one shall pass away. Yet with the adventure that I had undergone, there was nothing for it, and if that caused such great alarm, then I cannot deny that having such foresight is worth the gain of what I was compensated with.

One often finds and fishes for one's great love in their present life or reflects on missed opportunities in their past. Yet I, in the most unorthodox manner imaginable, did not set my cap for a man to fall in love with, nor desired one initially, but I did find him—in the future. In the very distant future.

By rights, when I discovered him, he was in the early prime of his life—and I had been deceased for over a hundred years.

Yet who was the culprit for such mismatch of man and woman, for it was not us. I can assure all that Mr. Fitzwilliam Darcy walked into the circumstances quite ignorant of the means that we had met and went out of it equally so.

No, the only culprit, the criminal of this situation—or the savior of our situation, was Time.

Time in all its strangeness.

Its unpredictable ways.

Its tricks.

And its traps.

Traps that no one can determine or explain.

Therefore, when I found myself where I was at last, where I met him as my distant future, and he looked on me as his distant past, there was room for only one thing initially: erroneous misunderstandings and pure discomfort.

And I suppose that Time, in all its power, had great amusement with us on the matter.

Yet I am getting quite ahead of myself, and unlike time, I ought to be linear rather than not so. Therefore, I shall begin a week before the day that all would change so irrevocably. I shall return to when I was in Hertfordshire, 1812, walking from Meryton, where I had just taken a stroll, to my home, Longbourn.

# Chapter One

## HAPPY NEWS IN HERTFORDSHIRE

A ll through town there was news and announcements given of an imminent conflict that was between England and our lost colonies, the United States of America.

The year marked many misunderstandings, or prideful actions of mistakes on both sides of the ocean, and I was not so proud an Englishwoman that I would deny this. And yet it all now had become quite certain. In my lifetime, at the firm age of 26, I was to see England once more go to war with America, and I rushed home to offer the news, hoping that my father had not read it in the newspaper first.

Walking at a brisk pace away from Meryton, I passed my Aunt Phillips along the way, who I knew to have just come from visiting my mother and she looked excitable, as always.

"Aunt Phillips, good day," I bade hello to her.

"Ah, Lizzy," she answered with a smile. "You find me coming from your mother, filling her with all sorts of good news."

"Good news?" I asked. "What sort of good is this news? The overwhelming kind? The lovely kind? Or the sensational kind?"

"All three, I can assure you, for it is the best news in the world."

Then she eyed me cunningly. "But I shall not tell you, Lizzy, for I know that your mother will wish to be the first one to do so."

Knowing this to be so, I answered, "Yes, I suppose that she will."

"Besides, I best be on my way, for as you know, Mrs. Goddard has just redecorated the walls of her sitting room, and she is wishing for my opinion on the wallpaper, and I figured that I might as well.

"As you know, she places much faith in my advice, but I really do wish that she had asked me for my advice before she had it put up. After all, how was I to—well, if you do think wisely on it, it would have been better to have—well, really, Lizzy, one should always ask advice about such permanent things as wallpaper before one puts it up." She made a tsking sound in her throat.

"Now I have no choice but to like it even if it is not pretty. Many wallpaper designs are—well, yes, they are. Quite bad! Indeed, quite bad! Only certain designs suit my—well, only certain designs. In my opinion, one ought to mostly just paint a room rather than put up paper, for it can easily fall apart—yes, quite so quite so, Lizzy. And she puts much stock in my advice. I do not claim to be an expert on anything, but often my friends simply do."

She continued on this way for quite some time, often telling me that she was in a hurry and then speaking on for another couple of minutes. After spending ten minutes in this manner, I finally had to disentangle myself from her company, using the excuse of needing to return home by a certain time so that I could be of use to my father, and at last we parted.

Aunt Phillips was the standard voluble aunt that one must and will always have in one's family. She loved to talk, both news and nonsense, and therefore, like my mother, she was a mixture of the rational and the ridiculous, and one always was amused of which side would be produced.

The rational side gave out the news. And the ridiculous side delivered the delightful gossip that kept my mother alive and happy. For, when a woman is married and has many children, busy work is her antagonist and news of other people's misfortunes is the balm that soothes the bruises that the dullness of everyday life gives her.

Therefore, on my way I went, and eventually I turned the corner and was walking down the lane to Longbourn where my home appeared on the horizon. I stopped a few feet away from it and leaned against a tree.

One day, this would no longer be our home, because an unfortunate entailment was attached to it, and since my father had no male heirs, we Bennet sisters were reminded daily of the fact that we must marry, to be forearmed against the worst!

Our mother would be sitting home, thinking of prescriptions to save us from losing our home if our father were to die, and each method our father would dismiss. Our lives were quite cyclical in that sort of way, but I still enjoyed it to a strange degree, for it left much for me to be amused by and laugh at in secret.

Ah! I gasped, with deductive reasoning, I determined what was the reason that my Aunt Phillips was so conspiratorial in her look. It was a matter of a prospect on the horizon. Indeed, she had discovered that there was news of some gentleman or other!

I would indeed bet my life that *that* was the motive behind her furtive looks—and why she believed that it made my mother happy.

There, adjusting my bonnet, I walked down the lane and entered Longbourn.

⚜

As I walked in, I was met by my younger sister, Kitty, as she rushed down the steps.

"Lizzy," she declared.

"Kitty, dear, do not run down the steps like that," I said. "You know that can be dangerous."

"Oh, do not be so afraid of everything." She uttered a dramatic sigh. "Fear of any risk of any kind is Mary's duty."

"What has you so excited?" I removed my bonnet as she bounded up to me.

"News from town. Aunt Phillips has just come, and she and mother sat in the parlor for a good hour all alone while Lydia and I were in the back, tossing horseshoes. Aunt Phillips has just left, and our mother has been fluttering about the first floor of the house and sent Betsy into town to order a haunch of pork. But she hasn't told Lydia or me anything yet. And Mary is upstairs." She rolled her eyes.

"She hasn't told you what Aunt Phillips told her?" I asked, interested. "That is quite unique. Yet if I know our mother, which I hope to, since she has been my chief character of study for these twenty years at least, I believe that she is doing this for dramatic effect. Also it is near the time of our mid-day meal, so she perhaps shall wait to tell us then."

"Well, if that is your assumption…"

I raised my eyebrows. "What else am I to think?"

"Do you think it's about a gentleman?" Kitty's eyes were bright with interest.

"I both hope and worry that it is such."

"Why worry so?"

"Because," I answered, "if it's an eligible man who has come, then our mother will pounce on him with a fury."

"And therefore chase him off as soon as he has introduced himself to us." Mary came down the steps holding some sheet music, for it was now time for her piano practice. "And you all wonder why I care little for the matrimonial state."

"Yes, we do wonder," Lydia cried, running in from the washing room. "Lizzy, has Kitty told you that mama is holding a secret?"

"Yes, she has."

"Well, I hope that it shall not be long, for I want to know now!" Typical of Lydia; she was always so impatient.

"Where is Jane?" I asked Mary as she passed me.

"I did not pay attention," Mary said, "but when last I spoke to her, she was in her room."

"Lizzy?" I heard our oldest sister call for me from another room. Then the door opened, and Jane appeared, holding her diary in her hand, looking serene and demure, as she always did, but even more so when she was writing.

❧

"Mama has been calling after you," she said, closing her diary. "But you need not worry, for I told her that you had gone on your daily walk."

"Why does she not know of my daily walk at this point?" I asked, removing my gloves. "I've only been doing it for over a year."

"Oh, it is just simply not her way to notice it, but she means well."

We were both interrupted when we heard Mary begin practicing at the pianoforte.

"Practice time," I said with a groan.

"Aye." Jane smiled at Mary. "Practice time."

"Oh, for goodness sakes, Mary!" I heard our mother cry from another room. "Must you do that every day?"

"A woman must practice," Mary replied, not fully loud enough for our mother to hear from the sitting room, "to achieve proper execution."

"Mary!" our mother cried, "Please, dear!"

Mary stopped playing and stood up.

"Very well," she said stiffly, "though it gives me little pleasure to not play at this time, still I can very much prefer the company of a book."

"Worry not, Mary," Jane said, "for our mother just wishes to have the proper moment to tell us what she likes to announce."

"Jane!" our mother cried from the sitting room, "Is that you?"

"Yes, Mama." Jane sighed complacently, then she gave me a look.

"She's about to ask you if you have seen me," I whispered to her.

"Do you think so?" Jane asked.

"Jane, have you seen Lizzy yet?" our mother exclaimed, to which I replied with a smile of triumph.

"Indeed, I told you," I whispered.

"Yes, mama," Jane responded, "for she has just come."

"Oh, good! Jane, Lizzy, and Mary, come in! Come here!"

I rolled my eyes as I joined my sisters.

"I met our Aunt Phillips on the road from Meryton," I informed Jane, "and I have an idea what our mother calls us in for."

"Such as what?"

"It has something to do with a man, for our mother always loves to assemble us for such news."

"Indeed, you are right," Jane said. "For I believe that she wishes to inform us of how Netherfield Park is let."

I looked at Jane in surprise.

"What?"

"Yes," Jane replied, "for I was told this secret by our servant, Hill, who heard of it from Miss Stetson, who works in Lucas Lodge, who spoke to Miss Chiltern, who works at the Oakstead home, and Mr. Oakstead is the assistant to the attorney who oversaw the negotiations of Netherfield Estate. And Hill learned through them, that Netherfield Park is let, and it's to a wealthy gentleman."

"And you have not told mother this?"

Jane eyed me conspiratorially.

"I thought it was in our best interest to not speak of it, for you know how mother loves to be the bearer of such news. So, it's best that I pretend as if I had never learned about it."

I looked at her, surprised. "Well, I never knew that you had a side for concealment in that manner."

"It's an action I only use when I wish to give her pleasure, of course, and never to be merely furtive," Jane explained. "Yet, unless I am very much inaccurate, I believe that is what we are about to hear."

The three of us went into the sitting room, and there were our youngest sisters, Kitty and Lydia, sitting down to a game of backgammon, our father sitting by the fire and reading the newspaper while our mother was fluttering about the room, her handkerchief in her hand.

When we entered, she ushered us in, with a busied air, her hands moving in many directions as we sat and prepared.

"Oh, Lizzy!" she scolded me as I placed myself near Jane. "You picked the most ill-timed moment to go for a walk."

"My dear Lizzy is quite insensitive to how she administers her walking time." My father chuckled from behind his newspaper. "She times them as ill as Kitty times her coughs and Mary times her piano playing—and Lydia times her talking overall."

"I do not cough for my own amusement," Kitty retorted, hurt.

"Practicing leads to an industrious mind as well as a lady being most accomplished," Mary replied dryly.

"La, if all people did not speak unless they had something to say," Lydia cried happily, "then the whole human race would lose the power of speech."

"A very good joke indeed, Father," I said, for I was not certain that any of my other sisters understood that it was meant as such. "Yet in the future, I shall walk for only a half an hour a day rather than a whole one, for I fear that I shall continue to cause a scandal in our home if I do otherwise."

"If you will, my dear, if you will," he replied, smiling at me, then he continued to read his paper.

"Oh never mind that!" Our mother sat down amongst us all and smiled giddily. "Girls, I have the most wonderful news that I have just made your father acquainted with. Indeed, it is the very best of news! Netherfield Park has been let at last!"

❦

In hearing her finally announce it, I turned to Jane, who suppressed a smile and then looked thoroughly surprised by this news.

"Has it been, Mama?" Jane asked.

"Yes, my dears, it has!"

"But what has that to do with us?" Lydia wailed. "For if a family moves in there, then they shall only benefit our society if they give a ball."

"Oh, to go to a ball!" Kitty cried, clasping her hands together. "What could be more delightful?"

"I bet that I shall dance more dances than you," Lydia boasted.

"Nay, I shall be the one to do so."

"Either way, it shall be quite clear that we both shall dance more dances than Mary," Lydia cooed.

"Lydia," I chided.

"Oh, you know it's true, Lizzy."

"Because I do not value the worthless actions at a ball to signify anything of substance or importance," Mary answered. "And I do so wonder at you both."

"Oh, hush you all, for you quite distract me!" Our mother fluttered her handkerchief in front of her. "Lydia, this news is advantageous to you all, because Netherfield Park is not let by a common family. Oh, no! Netherfield Park is let by a young man of large fortune. A *single* man, named Mr. Charles Bingley, from the North. It is said that he has an inheritance of 5,000 pounds a year."

"Is he handsome as well?" Kitty asked.

Our mother looked at her sternly. "Who cares for handsome—well, I hope that he is a little bit as such. Yet with an inheritance of that much, he ought to be so. Yes, I believe that he must be so. He must be the handsomest man in the world."

"For," I said, tongue in cheek, "it is a rule, as always, that looks must be directly in proportion to one's wealth. If he has 5,000 a year, then that must lend sparkle to his plainest feature."

Our mother dismissed my comment with a wave of her hand. "Still his plainest feature does not signify, for this is a grand thing for us. Rarely do such men come into Hertfordshire and rarely do they come within three miles of Longbourn. This is a fine thing! A fine thing indeed, is it not so, Mr. Bennet?"

Our father did not reply.

"Mr. Bennet!" she cried. "Lower that paper, or I shall rip it in half."

I sensed our father rolling his eyes before lowering the paper. He then gave our mother his slightly undivided attention.

"Sorry, my dear, I was just reading about how America and Britain are once more at war."

"Oh, yes, but we all saw that coming. Besides, this is Britain. It seems that we are always at war. Now back to important matters." Our mother brushed off his concern.

"Such as Mr. Bingley?"

"Yes, such as that."

Father tilted his head toward her. "Is it very much a fine thing?"

"Yes, it is…when you visit him," she replied, with sharpness.

"Oh my dear," he answered wearily, "have we not spoken of this before? I truly see no occasion to visit him."

"And once more, Mr. Bennet, you must visit Mr. Bingley directly when he comes, as one ought to do with any new neighbor of ours.

What do you think, girls?" Our mother swung around to face us. "Your father and I have been debating this for too long now, and since he has a will of iron, we must do our best to persuade him."

Our mother's chief attention turned to Jane and me. Ah, that was her design in waiting for us to be present; she wished for us to be able to persuade him against his course of action.

"Jane and Lizzy, speak to your father," she demanded. "For if he would have his way, you shall all die old maids, and then he shall be sorry."

"My dear, I'm right here," our father added, "why talk of me as if I am deaf or nonexistent?"

"You might as well be nonexistent with the lack of action on your part," our mother replied hotly. "For look, does it not occur to you, sir, that when you die, Mr. Bennet, our daughters shall be penniless and homeless, with your whole estate being entailed away to your ghastly cousin, Mr. Collins? Indeed, you cannot sit there in your armchair and pretend as if you have left our daughters to a grand inheritance."

"Oh, I do not know, fifty pounds a year can help an economical person go quite a long way," he replied evenly.

"Oh, Mr. Bennet, whoever could live with such?"

"Economical people," he stressed, folding his paper on his lap.

Our Mother threw up her hands. "Economical people and poor people are not one and the same, dear. Now Lizzy and Jane, will you not persuade him to visit Mr. Bingley when he comes?"

"Mama," Jane assured her, "I am certain that our father shall consider calling on Mr. Bingley as surely as he would call on any new neighbor of ours."

"Oh Jane, have you not been listening? You heard him yourself."

"Noted and heard," I replied. "But I am very much in agreement, Mama. It is therefore up to our father to determine his best course of action."

Our mother threw up her hands once again.

"Is the whole world against common sense all of a sudden? Oh very well, but if you all die old maids and we find ourselves living in a one room flat in London, with you all begging on the streets for shillings, then you know who to blame, and that person is not me."

Hill entered. "Excuse me, sir and ma'am," she said, "but luncheon is now served in the dining room."

"Oh, thank goodness!" Lydia cried, jumping up. "For I was just telling Kitty that I feel as if I haven't eaten for days."

"And yet you look as if you ate only five minutes ago, as always," Mary mumbled as she passed us, and we all went into the dining hall to eat.

At the table, I sat down next to Jane and the whole time our mother talked, imploring our father to visit this new Mr. Bingley who had come into the neighborhood, all the while mentioning his possibly close demise, stressing how we would be driven from our home and how she was doing everything in her power to save our family from destitution.

As she continued to go on and on, with our father not caring to heed her request to lift a finger to meet Mr. Bingley, I leaned into Jane and she whispered, "Do you think he already knew about Mr. Bingley's arrival in Hertfordshire?"

"Yes, I am sure of it."

"Ah, and do you think that he shall visit him?"

"Jane, I am surprised at you." I chuckled, repeating her question, "Do you think that he shall visit him? I am quite sure that he already has."

# Chapter Two

## THE OTHER GENTLEMAN

L ater that night, when it was time for bed, I bade goodnight to all my sisters, then went into Jane's room and sat down on her bed as she brushed her hair in the candlelight. As she did so, with her beautiful face eyeing herself in the mirror, then placing curling cloth in her hair, I smiled at her.

"I recall," I said, "when I was younger, that I used to envy your straight blonde hair."

"Did you?" Jane asked, smiling. "Well, I can finally confess that I always envied you for your thick dark curls. Curly hair always frames one's face better, and you naturally were able to achieve what I have to work for. You and I were both equal then. And who knows, Mr. Bingley might like thick brown hair, as men have been wont to do."

"What men love is what you naturally possess, and I naturally lack."

"Oh, dear Lizzy. You must not undervalue yourself or overvalue me. For when one does such, it never ends well, for either party."

I reached out and straightened the collar on her nightdress. "And what makes you determine so?"

"For it makes me worry that I shall disappoint you," she said with a smile. "And it makes me worried that you shall choose a man, when the time comes, who is not worthy of you."

"Oh, come now." I jumped up, went over to her chair, leaned behind it and looked upon us in the mirror. "You are quite five times better than all of us, and disappointing any has never been something you are capable of. And as for myself, you know my sentiments on the arts of matrimony. I shall not marry, unless I feel the deepest of attachments."

"As must I," Jane said, putting down her brush and taking my hand in hers. "Lizzy—ah, to marry for love!"

"Yes, to marry for love…but of course, steps must be taken before one must marry for love. First, we find a man quite eccentric enough to propose to us without a dowry, then he has to find us, and then, above all, he has to exist to begin with."

"I should so much wish to believe that there is a chance he is out there in the world, Lizzy." She sighed, looking at us both while we sat there gazing upon our reflections in the mirror. "I do so wonder—do you think that this Mr. Bingley shall be such a man?"

"He has Netherfield Park, but there is one problem."

"And what should that be?"

"He is one man. And we need two."

Jane laughed at this, then finished preparing her hair.

"And that there shall be one man in this world who shall be willing to have us is quite a miracle enough."

"Well, miracles shall have to multiply then." She smiled kindly. "For I wish to believe that there shall be luck enough for the both of us."

"Two Mr. Bingleys in this world? Who knows? Perhaps he has a brother." I stood up and prepared to leave.

"On the note of speaking of miracles, I bid you goodnight. Say a prayer for me, Jane, for there is such a man for you, but I doubt there shall be one for me ever."

"I do not believe so, Lizzy," she expressed. "I merely believe that he shall not be so easy to find. For very little ever is."

I kissed her and left her room, went to my own, and retired for bed.

꙳

Our father, as was his want, would prove to be among the earliest of those who waited on Mr. Bingley at Netherfield Park, but we at Longbourn would discover this in the most indirect of ways.

A few days later, as Jane and I were in the garden, planting seeds for our flower bed, Charlotte Lucas, my good friend, and her mother, Lady Lucas, appeared.

"Lizzy and Jane!" She waved to us. "I come with some news."

"Ah, if it's about the mysterious Mr. Bingley," I said, standing up and happy to see her, "never fear, Charlotte, for we have been informed."

"Oh, I come with even greater news than that."

"Greater news than a single man, of large fortune, coming into Hertfordshire? Be careful, for such news could make our mother die of ecstasy." I stood and brushed off the grass from my apron.

"No, rather, she shall be overjoyed at the matter."

"It is possible she may very well have a stroke from it, then," I added.

"Heaven forbid." Jane sighed, as Charlotte and I embraced.

"So," I said, "what is this news?"

"Well, apparently, there shall not be one eligible gentleman that has come into Hertfordshire."

"There's not?"

"No, for now, there shall be two."

꙳

"Two gentlemen?" our mother cried. When Lady Lucas and Charlotte paid their visit, we showed them in, much to the relief of our mother who never secretly welcomed Lady Lucas happily into her home unless she had news that could profit Longbourn. This day, because she and Charlotte were the bringers of good news, there was not enough that could be said for her.

"Indeed," Lady Lucas said. "For Mr. Bingley shall not be coming alone. From what Sir William has learned from meeting Mr. Bingley, he has reported that he is a most amiable young man."

"And handsome to be sure," Charlotte whispered to me.

I gave her a knowing look.

"And that Mr. Bingley comes with a slight company. Such a company includes his two sisters, with one sister's husband, and then there is a friend of his, a Mr. Fitzwilliam Darcy of Pemberly."

"Pemberly?" Our mother echoed. "Is it a large estate?"

"It is said that it is in Derbyshire and is a very large estate! And he has ten thousand pounds a year."

When this was uttered, we all opened our eyes in subtle shock— except for our mother—who was very vocal and physical in her reaction. She appeared as if she may have suffered from an epileptic fit suddenly and then she calmed down.

"Ten thousand a year?" she repeated, most excited. "That cannot be."

"Sir William has it upon good authority."

Our mother was all atwitter as she could barely contain her glee.

"Oh, even better and better, this Mr. Bingley brings good hope into Hertfordshire. Oh, if Mr. Bennet does not obey me and pay a visit to Mr. Bingley, I shall haunt him like a harpy filled with fury."

Lady Lucas and Charlotte looked at each other in confusion.

"But..." Lady Lucas started, "Mr. Bennet *has* paid a visit to Mr. Bingley."

"No, he hasn't," our mother objected. "You are mistaken, for he continues to demand that he has not."

"Mrs. Bennet," Charlotte said, "I hesitate to dispute with you, but my father, Sir William, returned home not four days ago and told us of how he paid a visit to Mr. Bingley and met Mr. Bennet there in the process of doing so."

When Charlotte reported this, my mother became quite flushed. Charlotte turned to me, made a humorous face and I returned it with one of my own.

"Mama," I began softly, "you may recall that our father merely jokes of such things, and no more."

Then, as if the mention of him was enough to summon him

forward, our father suddenly emerged from his library and he walked past the door.

"Mr. Bennet!" our mother cried.

Our father stopped and turned to us in the doorway.

"Oh, we have guests. Oh, and Lizzy, is that a new muslin gown, my dear?"

"It is, Father."

"I hope Mr. Bingley will like it, Lizzy."

"He would not see it since we would have never been introduced because you would not visit him," our mother cried. "But Lady Lucas has just informed me that I have caught you out in a lie, sir."

"Ah!" Our father sighed. "So I have been found out before I wished to be. How very unfortunate for my pride and my delicate scheming."

"Then…you have called on Mr. Bingley?" Our mother was incredulous.

"I have indeed! Really it could not be helped, try as I might. But I have actually paid the visit, therefore we cannot escape the acquaintance now."

"Who would wish to escape it?" Our mother laughed.

"Me, for I see that it shall cause many days of me hearing nothing else but this matter."

Our astonishment was just what our mother would have wished, including Lydia and Kitty, who had come in from the gardens when they heard that Lady Lucas was there. Only three of us Bennet sisters were calm and collected.

Mary was so because she did not care for such things.

Jane was so because it was just her natural way.

I was so because I was merely amused and self-satisfied. Jane and I had been correct, and our father had called on Mr. Bingley. Yet my inner peace of mind was such for more reasons than not.

Every woman in the room had already set their cap at the idea of thinking these two men to be the equivalent of white knights upon strong steeds, being the epitome of all that was gallant, romantic, and chivalrous. Yet long ago, I had learned that a gentleman was like any other. His breeches were breeches, his cravat was crisp, his vest would be well cut, his boots would be of the better brand, with his hair parted to the side. What did he present that no other man ever would or could? And therefore, I knew myself to be protected from making a man into a dream and being unable to separate the two from each other.

But that was not enough for Lydia and Kitty, who were now taking each other's hands and dancing around while our mother cheered out happily, adoring our father, which was quite new.

"Oh, I knew that I should persuade you at last, Mr. Bennet," she declared. "Yes, I was quite victorious, and all shall turn well by the end. And you did not tell us, making it quite the good joke."

"And I bet that there shall be a ball," Lydia cried. "Yes, I believe that there may be a ball perhaps."

"Lydia, my love, though you *are* the youngest, I dare say Mr. Bingley will dance with you at the next ball."

"Oh!" Lydia boasted, "I am not afraid; for though I *am* the youngest, I'm the tallest."

"Actually, I'm a couple of inches taller," Kitty announced.

"No you're not!"

"Yes, I am."

"No, you're not."

"Forgive my desire to settle the debate," I said, "but Lydia, indeed, Kitty has grown uncommonly of late, and now, she is the tallest of our lot."

"Oh, you are playing favorites…"

"Says the one who loves only herself," Mary said to Lydia, while leaning over her book.

"Oh, go write an extract of another conduct book that you don't even secretly agree with!" Lydia stomped her foot and then sat down in a huff. "Dear me, I do long for a dance of some kind. Well, now that we know that Mr. Bingley is available and ought to be our dream in every particular way, then I hope that he shall come to the Assembly Room next Saturday!"

"Oh, I am sure that he shall, my dears," our mother cried, merrily taking Lydia and Kitty's hands. "And you both shall be able to dance with Mr. Bingley."

"If he is the sort of man to ask a woman to dance," I added.

"Oh, nonsense child! What sort of man is there in the world who would not wish to dance with my daughters? No indeed, and then, there shall be this Mr. Darcy for you as well."

"Well," Kitty inferred, "I do not like uncertainties, so Lydia and I shall look forward to Mr. Bingley, and I leave it to Jane and Lizzy to charm Mr. Darcy."

"And we shall see Mary married to the wall," Lydia ridiculed.

"The wall will always be a more agreeable companion than anyone that you would set your cap at, Lydia," Mary said, "judging by your views and values. If you have any views and values."

"Yet for our part," Jane pressed, referring to what Kitty had said, "Lizzy and I surely do not intend to set our cap at either gentleman."

"No, but it is your mother's," our father said. "So be prepared to choose your wedding gowns by tomorrow morning."

"One should never choose one's wedding gown in the morning," I interjected, "for it is too early to make any rational decisions."

"Ah, now that was well put," my father complimented me, and I smiled, feeling his compliment.

# Chapter Three

## THE SOUND OF BELLS

As we sat there, with our mothers chattering away, Charlotte stood up, came over to me, and we took a turn about the gardens together.

"What do you think of this news?" Charlotte asked me, smiling. "Should we be excited for the one with 5,000 a year or the one with 10,000?"

"I find myself happy to be content with neither," I declared, "unless they meet the necessary requirements."

"And what are those?"

"They actually must like me in return," I said with a laugh. "For if not, then I cannot possibly think they are of sound mind or judgment, and you know very well that I can never grow fond of a man who is not sensible."

"Dear Lizzy," Charlotte Lucas chuckled, taking my arm, "you know, there is only one thing better than the prospect for two such men coming into Hertfordshire."

"And what would that be?"

"Three men," Charlotte said knowingly. "Three such men would always be better than two. This way, there would be a man for Jane, you and myself. And nothing could be more perfect, surely."

"You weigh much of our domestic joy on two men who I have not met yet. Are you wishing to have me stumble on assumptions?" I smiled and squeezed her hand. "For those are always the puddles on the road which one stumbles on."

"While I can see your reason to proceed with caution," Charlotte whispered, her shoulder against mine. "You know that I cannot afford to be romantic, so I must be economical. Three men coming into the neighborhood would increase my chances."

"But do you think these two men are even worth setting your cap for? For all their thousands of pounds a year does not render them less repulsive from having disgusting characters, then we must know of it before we even think to dream of them. To speak plainly, why fall in love with the idea of someone when there is the chance that he is not worthy of regard?"

Charlotte tilted her head to one side. "And we differ on this matter."

"Do we?"

"Yes, for in truth, happiness in marriage, I have always found, is entirely a matter of chance, you know. For when entering the marriage stage, most often both the man and woman deceive the other, showing their best sides. Therefore, if one's chance of being happy with a husband is just as much not likely as it is likely, then it is better, in my opinion, to know as little as one can about the defects of one's partner."

"You are speaking in jest, surely." I gave her an affectionate laugh.

"Oh, do I?" she said with a smirk. "Well, still as for this Mr. Bingley and Mr. Darcy... I wish Jane the best of luck, for we know who they shall set their cap for."

"Yes, I believe they will," I replied, looking at Jane fondly as she appeared in the doorway. My expression turned to one of temporary sadness, for in the matter of one second, I felt a slight bit of inadequacy. However, I was not very discrete in my look, because Charlotte discerned it and, being intuitive, took my hand in hers.

"Yet, Jane is not the only one blessed with such capabilities to attach a man to herself, for indeed, while Mr. Bingley may perhaps think she is the best—perhaps your fate may find itself on the path toward this Mr. Darcy."

"To this Mr. Darcy?" I laughed. "Now you really wish for me to live in dreams. Well, I thank you for it, because perhaps, dreams may be delightful to remain in every now and again. Yet, if Mr. Darcy falls in love with you, whatever sort of man he proves to be, then Charlotte, I promise that I shall be happy for you."

"As I said—why could there not be three men?"

"Well, perhaps there is a third man, and he simply has failed to appear. Dear me, I hope when he does come, that he proves not to be an idiot!"

We both laughed as we entered my home again and Lady Lucas stood up as their visit came to an end.

Once she and Charlotte had departed, our mother fluttered about even more, assuring Kitty and Lydia that Mr. Bingley was said to be a delightful man, that he would be willing to dance with them both, and that she was absolutely certain that they would find Jane to be the loveliest woman in the county!

And as usual, she said nothing to me—which I had grown mostly accustomed to. Jane eyed me with a slightly sympathetic look, indicating that she was aware of our mother's indelicacy toward my feelings. Yet time had hardened me towards it, therefore I was able to feel nothing else but amusement.

And then came the sound.

The sound of a clock.

Bells were chiming.

At first it was slight, and I looked toward our clock while doing so, but it had not hit the hour by any means, so there was no reason for why it would be chiming.

"Is our clock broken?" I asked out loud, and Mary, who had been sitting closest to me, was the only one who heard me.

"What?" She looked up from her book. "Beg your pardon?"

"The clock. The bells are chiming, and it has not even reached the hour."

Mary looked at me queerly.

"Elizabeth, what are you talking about?"

"The bells. Didn't you just hear them? They had gone off a second ago."

"No, they didn't," Mary said. "I heard nothing."

"You didn't?" I asked, utterly confused.

"No, Lizzy, I did not."

"But…" I stood up, walked over to Kitty, and then tried to appear nonchalant. "Kitty, did you just hear the bells on our clock ring?"

"The bells?" Kitty replied, looking toward the grandfather clock leaning against the wall. "Why would they ring? Clearly it is not the hour yet."

"Then—you did not hear anything?"

"No, Lizzy. Nothing at all." She eyed me closely, wondering if there was something the matter with me. Yet she was not alone. Why had I heard the bells on a clock when it was not possible to do so? There was nothing to account for it, but I was left with a desire to be alone.

"Elizabeth, are you quite well?" Kitty's voice interrupted my musings.

"Yes," I replied slowly. "Perhaps I am a little tired or need a little fresh air."

"Oh, I know what that means."

"What?"

"You are about to take a walk to the stream. That's what you always mean when you say, 'a little fresh air'," Kitty announced.

"Ah, I never knew my intentions were always so transparent. Thank you, for I must correct that in the future."

I stood up and excused myself, informing my family that I just wished for a little fresh air once more, to which my mother remarked that I walked too much, my father gave his permission without even listening to my mother, Lydia, Kitty and Mary did not care, and Jane offered to join me. I thanked her, but I decided that it would be best for me to walk about myself. Jane accepted this, but I could discern that she knew I was unsettled in some sort of way. However, I was quite determined, so I put on my bonnet once more, and walked out into the garden.

⚜

As I walked across our lawn, enjoying the prettiness of the wilderness that surrounded it, heading toward the shorter route towards the stream near Oakham Mount, I was left to the freedom of being able to consider what had occurred.

The sound of bells!

Bells from a clock, and yet I had been the only one to have heard them. Why could it be so?

All that there was to assume was that I must have been a little tired, and my imagination took control over me for a moment, for I felt a great deal better at that point.

Yes, a walk could always clear one's mind—therefore, what was there for me to assume about myself?

Why the sound of the chimes on a clock, for what was going on at the time to make my mind astir with wonder? It was talk. Talk of Mr. Bingley and also this Mr. Darcy that was to be in our midst. Such a subject matter was of little to no use to me, I knew this, for Jane, naturally possessing the most beautiful, gentle manners, and having the sweetest disposition between the five of us, would be expected to always be the one to capture the fancy of any gentleman who would find himself wandering into the wilds of Hertfordshire. This I had grown accustomed to.

And between Jane's superiority of looks, and Lydia and Kitty being great favorites of our mother, I was never to be thought of when it came to possessing the charms to win over any man of worth. Until now, I had never cared for such preferences. All in the household of Longbourn had their place, knew it well, and we clung to it. My talent, though it was not a generous one, therefore, you need not desire to covet it, was that my disposition was of such lightness that my spirits could recover from anything. As such, jealousy of any kind was something I was not oft to feel, until this circumstance.

Often my father's love for me softened the pains that I experienced at the hand of my mother's inability to favor me in any way. While my mother did love me, this was certain, it was an obligatory sort, where I knew her love, felt it on occasion, but then it was overlooked or lost under her favoring most of my other sisters over me. All I could deduce was that the result of this was that dear Jane was the oldest and had her love initially, and Lydia was the youngest, therefore my mother favored her as the baby of the family.

Yet therein lay another assumption that I made, and that was that I reminded her too much of my father. The relationship between our parents was one that presented a constant scene where both partners could not fully love and respect the other—thus it was not often agreeable to either party involved. Therefore, I suppose, when my father favored me, the disappointment that sprang within her of not often gaining my father's affection or his attention spread towards me, but I suppose that I would never fully know for sure.

Eventually I reached the stream and I took a few rocks and began to try and skip them—something I always lacked the talent in doing, yet I was still determined to do it.

After skipping my last rock, I felt my temper and vigor rise to what it once was.

My mother's tone and lack of consideration of me had quite done away along with any ill feelings, and my confidence was returned to its rightful place. Looking at the stream, I decided to indulge in an old pastime that I used to do, and wade in the shallow ends of the stream.

So I removed my shoes, stockings, placed them on the ground, lifted my petticoat and then I paraded into the water.

When we were children, Kitty and I had done it quite often when our mother had lost sight of us and believed us to only be playing in the yard.

"Well, mother." I laughed to myself. "You always say do not carry on in my wild ways. Here is where I can be nothing else except myself."

And then I heard the sound again.

The sound of the bells!

The bells of a clock.

At first, they rang faintly, as if I was hearing it from far off, at a large distance.

I took a few steps further into the water, still holding up my petticoat, and wondered at it.

"What is it?" I asked myself.

The sound ceased, and I was left in silence only briefly when I heard the sound of a clock bell ringing slightly louder this time. Thinking it was merely the actions of a joke or trick of some sort, I looked around.

"Kitty and Lydia! I know this must be you!"

Yet as I looked around, there was no indication that anyone was there, no sign of a petticoat hiding behind the trunk of a tree, or a bonnet in the branches. There was only me.

I feared that I was going quite mad, but I was not afraid at the moment.

The sound of the clock bell grew louder this time as it was getting closer and closer.

"What is it!" I cried to the air. Yet no voice returned to me but my own, and I was left to determine that I was having a hallucination of some sort. That was it! I was merely ill.

Turning around abruptly, I began to rush out of the water, but suddenly I was seized.

My foot was clearly caught on something, for I could not move it. I looked down through the water, expecting to see my ankle caught on an underwater root of some kind, or a fishing line that had gotten lost to the tide, but there was nothing. Nothing at all that I could see was tying me down in any small way, but I was caught nevertheless, and I attempted to pull myself free, yet my foot would not budge. It was as if I had been shackled down by cuffs of silver, and it merely was not visible to the eye. Then all of a sudden, I nearly stumbled in the water, for my leg was being pulled backwards, further back into the depths.

The sound of the bells was growing louder.

I steadied myself, trying to liberate myself from the invisible link that was pulling me—and only then did I begin to grow afraid.

The bell of a clock now was so loud that I could hear and attend to nothing else.

Whatever was pulling me had gathered strength, for its force had quite knocked me off my feet and I was now immersed in the water, grabbing at the ground as I still fought on.

Fear eclipsed all as I cried out, begging for help from the air or any that could hear me.

Longbourn was too far away! Too far for me to be saved by Jane or Kitty! Too far to have a chance, but still I had to save myself.

*Elizabeth Bennet! You must save yourself!*

Onward I struggled, but the sound of the clock bells now came to an end, and it was altered, to the sound of a large clock ticking away.

Tap. Tap. TAP. TAPPP!

The sound of a clock hand's moving on, indicating the rise and fall of a minute grew louder and louder, making me desire to believe that I was in the midst of a nightmare.

Yet it was all too real. My skin was cold, and I was wet all over. Fear gripped me as, with my last breath, I was completely submerged underwater in the stream, being pulled by the invisible force.

When fear takes one, when it grabs at every part of you, you can think of little else, but only the terror. When I had been taken underwater, I had my mouth open and therefore I felt my chest tighten as the air in my lungs was leaving me, and it was agony.

I flailed my arms, folded my body in the water and wrapped my hands around my ankle, trying to find what restrained me, but there was nothing! How could nothing and everything grab me all at once?

The agony in my chest reached its peak as I began to weep underwater. This was the end for me—the very painful and bitter end that I had never thought.

There was so much that I had not accomplished.

No, I did not wish to go.

I could not leave Longbourn!

And my father and mother would never learn what had happened to me.

Kitty.

Lydia.

Mary…

And Jane!

Dear Jane, one of my greatest of friends and favorite of sisters!

And Charlotte Lucas.

Eventually, over all the pain, I felt my life leaving all of me as I began to drown in full, and with my lungs filled with water, I sunk further and further down—further than I ever believed the stream to have been, and then my eyes closed.

# Chapter Four

## STRANGE NEW WORLD

And then, when all hope had faded, I felt my foot release!
With this new burst of freedom, I opened my eyes, and yet, my strength was quite done away since I had so little air in my lungs. However there came the impulse to live—deep within, the impulse still remained.

To return to Longbourn!

To see my family once more.

Therefore, I opened my eyes and I struggled to live as I saw the surface of the water. Yet here was the strange thing! With there being so little air in my lungs, I had become quite delirious, it was apparent, for there felt as if there was no bottom to the stream, and instead, the water was dark, and appeared to be endless. Up ahead, I saw a large bottom to something that appeared to be a boat—yet it could not be.

From the clock to this new…image I was only imagining things, and no more.

'Jane, Kitty, Mary, Lydia, mother and father—may you be my incentive,' I prayed, 'and my strength.'

Pushing forward I began to swim to the surface that was higher than I had recalled it to be, and then I burst through into the air.

Gasping for breath, my back arched as I took in the most welcome air. It was a blessing—a great one!

I was alive, and now I could return to Longbourn at last. Oh dear, Mama would be so angry, and Jane would be worried, but Father, Kitty and Lydia would only laugh. I had no knowledge of what Mary's reaction would have been, but it would be something that would attempt to be smart, but not fully being so.

Now that I was alive, I did find the significance behind a joke, and now it was time to—

The light and air had distracted me. For once I had become accustomed to the illumination, I saw that I was in no stream, nor was the bank anywhere to be seen.

Fear and panic gripped me when I realized that I was in the midst of a large river, and the bank was clearly far away!

"My god! Where am I?"

"There's a woman there!" I heard someone shout. I turned to who called out and realized that what I had seen underwater was clearly a boat! A boat that was the size of a ferry—perhaps that was precisely what it was—but it was the strangest ferry I had ever seen. It was white, was strangely designed, but there were people who were peering at me treading so vigorously in the water.

The person who had seen me was a little girl, and she was the one who was pointing towards me and pulling at her mother's dress.

"A woman, a woman in the water!" she repeated, to which the cries of the rest of the people followed as they pointed at me. And then I saw a shadow behind me as they all roared out.

"No! Watch it, there is a woman in the water, below your ship!"

I turned and saw that the shadow that loomed over the water behind me was no cloud of any kind, but to my horror, it was one of the largest ships that I had ever seen.

And it was coming right towards me.

I cried out, but refusing to panic, I turned around and began to swim as quickly as I could in the opposite direction of the ship, but as I continued to swim, I saw a strange sort of fanning 'tool' under the ship that was moving at quick speed, and I deduced that somehow, it was propelling the ship forward. I knew not what it was, but there was too much strangeness occurring at once to think or consider anything properly.

Yet, with the speed that I had to comprehend anything, I must be in London, in the Thames. Though how I arrived there, I knew not. All that mattered at the moment was that I escaped from the onslaught.

Therefore, swimming forward and feeling the presence of the boat nearby, I still heard the sounds of the cries from the ferry, trying to urge the ship to come to a halt to keep from sailing over me—and if it did not, it would overtake me. I knew it. I was certain of it.

I was about to die.

❦

And yet I did not. For I suppose, while I very vigorously swam forward, the ship must have finally come to a halt, for I did not feel or hear the boat drawing any closer to me.

Finally, I grew so tired that I ceased to swim, and I paddled there, giving my limbs a moment to relax. Gathering my courage, I turned around, looked to see that in fact the ship had quite slowed down and the men on the deck were now looking down at me.

"What the hell are you doing in the water?" one of them shouted in such a rude manner and in an accent I barely understood.

"I don't know!" I cried, suddenly annoyed with him. "Do you think I meant for this?"

"Come closer!" came the demand from the ferry driver. I turned as some man who was clearly giving announcements on the boat, raised a strange instrument to his mouth and talked into it. "We're going to sail closer to her!" he boomed, and his voice was very loud as he spoke into this instrument. "Just to get her."

"That's fine," the man on the ship said, for the ship was five times the size of this strange white ferry. I was very grateful as the ferry sailed towards me and I also swam to it.

Once it got close enough, I saw that the ferry announcer wore a lime green shirt that was strangely buttoned. He wore a strange hat as well, with some very different breeches. For goodness sakes! What was happening in London that we were never informed of in the country? How had the fashion changed so utterly without it never being posted in any gazettes?

As the man looked at me, he removed a rope from the side and lowered it down to me.

"I thank you!" I cried, taking it and then grasping it tightly. "Forgive me, but I cannot climb it. I do not know how to attempt it."

"Don't worry," he replied, again with an accent, "we're gonna pull you up."

Some more people rushed to assist him, and they pulled me out of the water. When they did, and helped me over the edge, I noticed the little girl who had spotted me in the crowd. I smiled at her as she rushed forward with a small light jacket of hers.

"Do you need my jacket?" she asked innocently. "Because you're really wet."

"Thank you," I said, "but I am afraid of leaving a water mark upon it."

"Don't worry," the ferry announcer said, getting some blankets from a bag he had. When he took it up, he offered it to me. I thanked him greatly and wrapped myself in them.

"I cannot thank you enough for your kindness," I said, but he, the boat driver, and the rest of the people on the ferry were looking at my bonnet and clothing very pointedly.

"Oh, are you one of the historic reenactors?"

"I beg your pardon?" I asked, confused.

"Your costume? The dress and the bonnet? Are you one of the historic reenactors who play a historic character in Old City?"

While I was quite grateful to them for saving me, I could not understand a thing he was on about, and much less the strange way he spoke.

"I'm afraid that I do not have the pleasure of understanding you," I replied. "But I wear no costume, for I am no actress! I merely wear the fashion that is proper for our—"

Then I listened to them all and realized that they sounded distinctly different than anything I ever heard. And the way they were dressed was so very strange and inappropriate. I even saw quite a few young women wear short breeches—and breeches on women!—and then I also saw some wear shifts and chemises as outerwear! And the men, well I couldn't even define what they were wearing.

"You do not sound like Londoners," I said, "but then, I am not in London, am I?"

They all looked at me strangely, and then the boat announcer blinked.

"Are you joking?"

"Indeed, I am in earnest. Is this not London?"

"London, England?"

"Yes."

"No, this is not. You're in America."

"I'm what?"

"You are in the Delaware River now, and this is Philadelphia."

🐚🦋🐚

"Philadelphia?" I blinked, utterly confused. "Philadelphia, Pennsylvania?"

"Yes."

"As in the city of the revolution? The American Revolution!"

"Yes," the driver said, puffing out his chest with pride. "If that's what you think of it."

"Oh, my god!" I wailed. "It cannot be."

How did I get here? And what's more, I was an Englishwoman in the beating heart of the country that my nation was now back at war with. Our second war had begun, and now they would think I was nefarious for some reason for being here! I was in a dangerous place.

A woman came forward on the boat and looked upon me as if I was a spooked animal. "You don't know where you are?"

"No, I do not!" I nearly wept. "And I don't understand. I was in England."

"When?"

"A second ago, I was in England."

They all looked at each other once more, and then another woman stood up and rushed toward me.

"She clearly must be ill in some way," she declared. "Here, I'm a doctor, let me look at her."

She came toward me, leaned down, opening a bag that she had with her, then she smiled at me. "Don't worry, I won't hurt you."

While she said so, I still had the impulse to recoil, so she moved slowly.

"Don't worry. I just have a couple of items with me that can check your pulse, your eyes and your general appearance."

"But…you're a doctor?"

"Yes," she said, taking something out of her pocketbook. "That's the thing with being a doctor. We learn very soon after we get out of school that it's best to always carry some equipment on us." She picked up a small object, it projected a light from it, and she informed me that she was going to inspect my eyes. I let her do so, marveling at her actions.

"You say that you are a doctor?" I repeated, utterly amazed.

"Yes," she replied, still flashing the light over my eyes.

"But—women are never doctors."

"What?" She stared at me, confused. "What do you mean?"

"Women are never doctors. It's not a profession that is available unto us."

"What the hell is going on over there in England?" she asked, shrugging her shoulders, continuing her inspection. "Your eyes are not dilated or enlarged in any way. Therefore, it is clear that you are not under the influence of any drugs or narcotics. Now, I shall check your pulse."

She used some sort of object that I had never seen before.

"What is that?" I asked her.

"A stethoscope," she replied, looking at me again strangely. "What? You've never seen one before?"

"No."

"Really?"

"No, I haven't. What does it do?"

"It helps me hear your heartbeat," she answered slowly, "to make sure that your heart is beating at a normal pace. Also I check your lungs."

"You can check my heartbeat that way?" I asked, amazed. "You are in earnest?"

"Yes. And it's beating fine, just a little fast, but that's clearly from all the excitement. Now I must check your temperature."

"And what is that?"

"It's a thermometer."

"A ther…"

"Mometer. A thermometer."

She checked it and said that I was slightly feverish, but nothing to cause alarm.

"But if you are recovering from a larger fever before this," she said, "then it can explain a great deal."

"How so?"

"Because high fevers cause hallucinations. You could have been suffering from such."

In hearing her say this, I felt instantly better. Perhaps I had a fever. And perhaps this all was merely a hallucination still! Yes, that was it and no more. I was in the midst of a dream, and therefore all was left to do was wake up. In all my years, I had never learned how to escape a dream, for from what I recalled, one never knew one was dreaming when one dreamed. Yet I suppose there was always a first time for everything in life.

Unfortunately for my part, I never mastered the idea of how to waken myself, therefore there was nothing else left to do but for me to continue on until something woke me. Yet, now knowing that it was a dream and no more, I felt more comfortable and more accepting of whatever absurdity was presented to me.

People in strange clothing: well, perhaps it was something I ate.

A strange ferry: there is more of gravy than grave about that concept.

Women as doctors: clearly a secret wish of mine that had re-established itself in my subconscious. Yes, it was all a dream.

⚜

I nodded my thanks to the doctor, but she was not finished.

The ferry driver had begun to turn on the boat once more and we continued to sail along the water. I did not know how one could just turn on a ferry in such a way, but after all, this was a dream, and in a dream, all was possible.

"Now," the doctor continued, "tell me, have you taken any medication of any kind in the last 24 hours?"

"No, I have not."

"How about the day before? Sometimes a drug can take a longer time to take effect in a negative way."

"No—Oh, but yesterday, I did have a headache. So I did take a little bit of arsenic to soothe it."

"What!" Everyone on the deck stated together, and the doctor looked at me as if I had slapped her.

"I beg your pardon, what did you say?" she asked.

"Well, naturally, I took a little bit of arsenic."

They all looked utterly shocked.

"How are you alive?" the green-shirted ferryman asked me.

"Of course I'm alive." I laughed, amused that I had shocked them in such a way, for it felt quite nice, for it to be so for the first time and not the other way around. "After all, it is only arsenic. Who doesn't use it for headaches?"

"Everyone doesn't!" the ferryman roared. "Because it's poison."

"What? No, it's not." His answer stunned me.

"Yes, it is," the doctor murmured. "It very much is poison."

"But...but...we all use it often and it has profitable results," I explained.

The doctor gave me a decisive look and then put her items back in her bag.

"Please get this boat to the shore fast," she ordered to the ferryman. "I need to get this woman to a hospital quickly."

36

❦

I didn't understand the need to have me taken to a hospital, but the woman seemed quite insistent, and perhaps that would be the place through which I would finally wake up at last. Therefore, I was optimistic on the matter and anticipated being taken to safety.

When the people asked me of how I got to the middle of the Delaware River, I simply told them the truth that I had been wading in a stream, suddenly I was taken underwater, and then found myself in the middle of the river. They looked at me as if I was mad, yet if I were to be taken to an asylum in the end, what harm could it cause?

The more I spoke, the more the doctor clearly believed that I needed medical assistance. But I did not believe I was in any danger, so I told her of the clocks, the sound of the hands ticking away, everything.

Eventually, the boat reached the shore and then I was in for an even greater surprise, for as it reached the docks of the river, somehow, the ferry turned into a vehicle of some kind. I couldn't see below it, but we went from sailing on water, to riding along onto a street.

"How is this boat doing this?" I shouted, leaning over the edge. But I saw no horse pulling it, only some strange black wheels. "And what are those?"

"Either you are delusional," one of the other passengers said, "or you are a method actor who is too much into her character right now."

"What's a method actor?"

"Never mind, you're delusional."

"Be kind to her," the doctor said, "for she clearly doesn't know what's going on." She turned to me. "Miss, this boat is a part of a company, and what's special is that these boats where tourists get on to see the water, are recycled army boats and they can morph from being a boat to being a truck."

"A truck?"

"Yes, a truck... a vehicle, an automobile that we ride along streets."

"Like a carriage?"

"Yes, like a carriage."

Eventually, we pulled along a road, and I gasped as I beheld the city of Philadelphia before me. How could my imagination have thought of any of this? There was no city in my life that I ever had seen resemble this! And yet, my mind clearly was being overstimulated.

Perhaps the doctor was correct. Maybe arsenic did have some repercussions that I was unaware of, and I would explore this in further detail later.

The tour guide—I learned his title when he informed me of it— was named Jake. The doctor's name was Clara Hoover.

The vehicle stopped off at the final destination at street signs that read 6$^{th}$ and Chestnut Street. It was a busy street, where there were many people dressed in this strange manner, and I looked around at all corners of the place. There was a building to the left that had a bell in it, another corner with a building that read 'Wells Fargo', and then there was another building across from us that looked closer to what I would expect the real Philadelphia to look like if I ever were to wake up and visit it.

"What is that building there?" I asked Doctor Hoover, pointing to it.

"Oh, that's Independence Hall."

"Independence Hall?"

"Yes, it's where the founding fathers of America organized the second Continental Congress in 1776 and they signed the Declaration of Independence."

"Wait." I recognized the famous/infamous act that much of my country still moaned over every now and again, stating that it was the Declaration of the biggest overreaction to grievances ever. "I heard of this building, and wasn't it called the Pennsylvania State House?"

"Oh, it was," Tour Guide Jake said, helping me down from this carriage thing. "It was originally called that, but after we won the Revolutionary War, it was called Independence Hall."

"Oh, well…" I trailed off as I looked around at all the strange carriages that were rushing along the road. Then I did see some real carriages nearby, that were stationed a block away, for anyone to pay for a trip, it seemed. But all around me, I was positively flabbergasted at everything I had seen. Indeed, I was feeling more and more as if I had strayed into a nightmare rather than a fascinating dream.

Across the street, I saw a woman standing on the corner with three children beside her, and they were all eating ice cream on cones. Seldom did I get the chance to partake in ice cream, but I could not help but stare at it for a time. I suppose, it was because it was something that felt like it was quite familiar.

The woman turned her head, and the little boy, not noticing what he was about, decided to walk into the street. I did not know much of what this dream of mine was conjuring, but I clearly saw that the traffic of the *carriages* was going opposite the direction he was walking.

The boy walked into the street while these strangely shaped carriages were heading straight for him.

Even if it was a hallucination or a dream that I was a slave to, I felt the urge to protect him still, for nothing could hurt me. Therefore, I cried out for him to go back as I rushed into the street in hopes of grabbing him.

I had been able to lift him up, but I heard a screech and turned to see a carriage contraption attempting to halt as it came towards us. Realizing that I could not get the boy and me to safety quickly enough, I pushed him toward the walk, away from the collision, and then I felt a sharp pain as this carriage crashed into me.

The pain was utter agony!

I felt my body rise, then I rolled onto the carriage window, the carriage halted, I rolled off it, and then fell hard onto the ground.

Every part of me felt bruised as my vision began to darken.

I heard the opening and closing of a door, and then the sun above me was blocked from my view as the face of a man appeared in front of it.

"Oh dear god!" he cried. "Are you badly hurt?"

"I…" I whispered, my voice hoarse, "I am…"

"Never mind. Do not speak. I'm calling an ambulance now."

The sun was even more blotted out as Dr. Hoover's face appeared next to his.

"Let me look at her!" she demanded, then she cradled my face in her hands.

"I didn't mean to, I swear," he murmured. "She was trying to save the boy and I couldn't stop quickly enough."

"I know," Dr. Hoover replied. "Call Jefferson Hospital, because it's only a few blocks from here, so an ambulance can get here fast. Also, that's where I work."

"Right...uh, do you know it's number?"

She gave him a set of numbers, then she ordered him to help lift me and pull me off the road.

Every part of my body ached as they relocated me, and all while they did so, I could not understand.

Dreams never hurt. They could scare, gladden, or confuse one, but this was the reverse. Indeed, this was not so, but instead this was something else. It made me question it for the first time; could this all be real?

For, with the little that I knew...only reality ever hurt this much.

Once they got me off the road, and this horrible day was coming to a culmination, I felt many people rush around me as the man laid me down. I tried to get a good look at him, but my vision was too blurry. For some reason, I wished to know who he was, therefore, with my last strength and through much effort, I opened my mouth.

"Who are you?" I inquired, my voice losing its strength as my vision suddenly grew utterly dark.

"I...forgive me. And my name is Fitzwilliam Da—"

I could not hear the rest. All went black, and I could recall no more as I had fainted.

# Chapter Five

## THIS NEW ACQUAINTANCE

At first the world came back to me in sounds. I heard a voice. A distinct voice.

Then slowly I opened my eyes and saw a blinding light, which took me a moment to adjust to. After blinking a little while, I saw shadows, shapes, and outlines of people.

There was no one in the room with me—and what a room it was.

It was white—very white. The air felt crisp, and clean. Air always felt clean in the country of course, but this was a strange sort of clean, as if it was superficial in some way. Around me there were strange items, machines of a foreign nature, and I was in a bed, for I was lying down, covered with a white blanket, and I was staring down at my feet. I leaned forward, but my body ached still. It was then that I saw that I had bandages on my stomach, arms, and forehead.

I ached everywhere; from my head to my feet there was a dull pain. As I attempted to get used to my surroundings, I realized I had no choice but to comprehend that I had not woken from my dream. The crash was not enough, nor the fear of death, for I was still caught—still laying asleep somewhere where my imagination ran wild.

Once I had taken in my surroundings, and the disappointment that they caused, I was attentive to the voices of the men outside of the room.

"I don't even know who she is," the first man said. "She passed out after I climbed from out of my car."

"From the reports of Dr. Hoover," came the other voice, "her mind was in a strange state beforehand. She was mentally distraught. Is that why she ran into the street?"

"No, she ran after a child who had gotten away from his mother," another voice corrected him.

"Oh. Well, luckily, she has no mortal injuries of any kind. There was a little bit of internal bleeding in her intestines, also a couple of her ribs are cracked, she has some strain on her arms as well, some cuts and bruises on her face, but in a few weeks, she shall recover."

The second voice I couldn't identify, but the first voice was familiar enough. Yet what was even more welcoming was the fact that his accent was similar to mine. Indeed, he was from England. It belonged to the man who accidentally hit me. Recalling it with perfect clarity, I did my best to remember everything he uttered before I fell away. And his name, it was…

"Fitzwilliam!" I exclaimed at the revelation, but it was too loud to not be marked, for the two men outside of the door immediately were hushed, and I saw their shadows as they stood there—stock still.

Then one shadow moved and entered the room. He was wearing the strange trousers, shirt and cravat that I had spied other men wear, and a white coat over that. The white coat was familiar enough—he was a doctor.

"Good afternoon, miss, I am Dr. Aleck Kennex. How are you feeling?"

"I…" I said, trying to sit up.

"Oh, no please remain there, for it shall hurt to move yourself." He pulled up a seat and sat down next to me, took my hand and I realized he was taking my pulse, as the other doctor had. "You've had a very interesting morning."

I winced as pain recurred in my head. "That's an interesting word for it."

Dr. Kennex chuckled and pulled a small board with paper on it, and I recognized it.

"Ah! Is that a journal of some kind?"

"Yes," he replied, eyeing me curiously, "it's called a clipboard."

"Oh, right. Forgive me, but where am I?"

"This is Jefferson Hospital."

"Oh, that's where Dr. Hoover works, is it not?"

"Yes, she does. She came in with you, but she's a maternity doctor, so that's why she did not participate in your operation. Forgive me, but you have been unconscious for five hours."

"Five hours!" I inhaled sharply.

"Yes, but all will be well, and while we had to operate on you without your consent, it was best to do so without further delay. There was much internal bleeding that had to be attended to. So, now, I must ask you of any allergies that you may have, and your medical history. What is your Health Plan?"

"Health Plan?" I asked, confused. "What are you referring to? For, I am afraid, I do not have the pleasure of comprehending you."

He gave me a puzzled look. "Surely—or do you have no healthcare plan?"

"I don't even know what that is," I admitted.

"Ma'am, they have Health Plans in England."

"If they do, then I have been misinformed for quite some time, and I do not consider myself as ever having such."

I looked behind him and on the other side of the door, I still saw the shadow of the man who had hit me.

"I know you're there," I said to him, very much unafraid. "You are Fitzwilliam. I heard that part. Your name is Fitzwilliam."

I heard the man inhale, and then slowly he entered the room.

Tall and strong he appeared. His hair was a dark brown, his eyes, as he neared me, were a cloudy gray. Yet his countenance was not something I could fully judge, because it belonged to a man who I could not analyze when I first looked upon him. It was clear that he did not know how to approach me. In his eyes, there was not a vacancy, but there was a sternness—or a timidity that was masked by strong and defined features. Was he angry with himself for almost hitting me? Was he angry that this had all happened? Did he blame me? Or was he ashamed? I truly could not tell you what his intention was, or his emotion behind it. For it masked much.

Eventually he neared the end of my bed, and his tall frame, his sturdy but slender countenance unnerved me slightly, and then he opened his mouth.

"Sorry for remaining back initially. I, um, I didn't—I worried that I would not know how to approach the situation. I apologize for hitting you with my car."

"With your what?"

"My car?"

I looked between him and Dr. Kennex.

"What do you refer to when you say a car, sir?"

"The—the vehicle I hit you with. My car?"

I thought on the strange carriage that he collided into me with.

"Oh, that is what my subconscious is calling it." I sighed, exasperated. "Well, fine, then it shall be a car."

The man and Dr. Kennex looked at each other oddly and then they turned to me.

"I beg your pardon?" the man named Fitzwilliam asked. "Oh, but you must be a little disoriented. Yes, I suppose that it is my fault."

"No, it was merely an accident," I replied, "and even I must admit to this. The little boy ran into the street, I ran after him and you did your best to avoid it all. You are no villain, sir, as I am no imbecile. Or at least, I am not an imbecile over this." I laughed sadly.

"Of course you are not," Dr. Kennex replied. "That little boy's mother wished to thank you a great deal. If it weren't for you, she wouldn't have a child anymore. Making you a hero then, and no good deed goes unpunished. And Mr. Darcy here, well, he along with Dr. Hoover, immediately called an ambulance to have you brought to the hospital as quickly as possible."

"Mr. Darcy?" I said, turning to the man standing at the foot of my bed.

"Yes, my name is Fitzwilliam Darcy."

"Mr. Fitzwilliam Darcy." I sighed, then closed my eyes, trying to weave all this nonsense into one frame—now I saw what my mind was doing. "Of Pemberly."

When I spoke this, the man, Mr. Darcy, leaned down and looked at me.

"You know about Pemberly?" he asked.

"Indeed, I do, because you are about to arrive in the county where I live. This is my mind creating a series of strange incidents of a disoriented reality where I dream up this horridly unreal place. It shall symbolize how your arrival feels as if it shall change everything." I stopped for a moment, as my strength had not yet returned.

"Forgive me for I tire of just going along with my dreams, and since we are trained to believe that dreams can sometimes hold an important message to reality, I now have learned the lesson."

I glanced up at him. "The lesson is that the arrival of you and Mr. Bingley might intimidate me because you shall cause chaos in your wake. But since I keep surviving everything, my courage shall rise with every attempt to intimidate me, and I should not be alarmed." I winced as a brief pain shot through my body.

"In fact, after all this, I doubt anything can unnerve me now. And I suppose that was the main lesson. I am Elizabeth Bennet, and I can stand against anything if I choose. I confess that I believed that dreams didn't ever feel nearly this painful or real, but one never knows that one is in a dream when one has it. I dearly wish to wake up, but I suppose that I must walk down this path until sunrise."

When I finished my speech, both Mr. Darcy and Dr. Kennex looked at me strangely, then Mr. Darcy turned to Kennex, worry etched on his features.

"Dear god, I've damaged her mind!"

"We checked," Dr. Kennex said, looking into my eyes, and then seemed to check some papers in a file on the clipboard. I squinted to see clearly, and I was a little disturbed to see that the paper was clear, and it had a strange imprint of a brain on it.

"And from what we could tell, there was no real sign of damage. Her mind appeared to be fully intact."

"What is that?" I asked.

"Oh, this is an x-ray."

My look of confusion said it all.

"An x-ray," he explained, as if he were reading me instructions of a certain stitch. "It shows me a blueprint, a map, if you will, of your mind. See, look at it."

He showed it to me, and I was amazed. "You can take portraits of my brain?"

"Yes."

I shook my head, clearly perplexed. "This is beyond me. Truly, how could I have thought of this?"

Dr. Kennex exchanged looks with Mr. Darcy, but I was quite vexed at that point, so I handed him the x-ray image quickly.

"Because it is," I confirmed. "My mind is not broken in any way. It's just the situation that is all in error."

"Mr. Bingley?" Mr. Darcy whispered, eyeing me dubiously.

"Yes?" I asked.

"You mentioned Mr. Bingley?"

"He's your friend, is he not?"

"Well, no...not a Mr. Bingley."

I attempted to sit up in bed. "What do you mean by that?"

Mr. Darcy's eyes darted back and forth, then he muttered, "Nothing. Nothing at all."

A voice without pretense, or any sense of well-concealed deception; his tone gave him away—he was holding something from me. He was lying. Yet I cared little, so I turned from Mr. Darcy and focused on Dr. Kennex.

"And also," I continued, "like Mr. Darcy here, I may be English, but I see by your treatment of him that you understand not to arrest me under the accusation of being a spy. This all may be a dream, but I still would not like to be thrown into a prison while I am injured. Even in my mind, I do not think that would be pleasant."

"A spy?" Mr. Darcy asked.

"Sorry, I am being quite testy. It is merely in response to the war between our countries."

"What war?"

"Did my mind forget that when in the arms of slumber?" I asked, in jest. "The war between America and England. Our second war has just been waged. Well, I shall play along. I am no spy. The petticoat is no ruse in any way, for I know how you must view us all as being nefarious."

"The second war?" the doctor asked, confused.

"Yes, we are at war again."

"Miss Bennet," Mr. Darcy began, his eyes sharp as a hawk's. He took a step forward, his brow arched in concentration, and his shoulders drooped, as if he was attempting to get closer to me. "With this war—are you referring to the second war between America and England, called The War of 1812?"

"We already are calling it that?" I asked, sarcastic in tone. "Dear me, we wasted no time with the title of it. After all, it is not even the next year yet. How do we even know if this war shall last long enough to be considered a full war when it has just begun?" I squirmed, uncomfortable.

"It may only last a couple of months before we either lose or regain our colonies. Forgive me, Dr. Kennex, and take no offense, but really, America never should have revolted in the first place. There was no need, really, for look, here we are, at it again. Dear me, I truly mean not to offend you."

The Doctor only looked at me, frozen, and I worried that my wild tongue had gone too far ahead of me in that instant.

"I just merely think that it would be best for the lands to merge once more," I explained, "that is all. One is always stronger together than divided, or is that what this dream is about? Dear me, this is getting all so very perplexing."

"Miss Bennet," he said, "I…what year do you think we are in?"

"1812 of course. What? Does my dream deny this now?"

Mr. Darcy bit his lip and looked quite uncertain.

"Miss Bennet," Dr. Kennex began, "when you were brought in, Dr. Hoover advised me that you were a little disoriented, but we have tested your blood and you have shown no signs of narcotics, substance abuse, or anything of that nature to cause alarm. But she said that you did prescribe yourself arsenic to relieve a headache yesterday?"

"What?" Mr. Darcy asked, confused. "Arsenic?"

"It was a diluted form," Doctor Kennex said. "For it has clearly not harmed her, and, from the little research I was able to do since her arrival, certain diluted forms of arsenic were used, as an ancient remedy, for headaches."

The doctor looked once more at me. "It was popular in the 18th and early 19th centuries. Now, I have never heard of it causing amnesia in any way, but that, mixed with something we cannot identify must be affecting your mind, Miss Bennet."

"No," I denied. "It's because this is all a dream, and you cannot convince me otherwise. I have taken nothing to affect my mind in any negative way."

"Miss Bennet, you are not—"

"Forgive me, doctor," Mr. Darcy interrupted, "but I must ask her something first before you continue. Miss Bennet, may I call you Elizabeth?"

"It is not precisely proper, but I shall allow it, for this is a dream."

"Elizabeth," he said heavily, "you said that you knew my name from its connection to Pemberly?"

"Yes, I heard of it. It is your home."

"Where is this home located?"

"In Derbyshire. Or that is what I was informed of."

Deeply affected by my words, he nodded. "It used to be."

"Was, sir? I heard that you were the proper master of it at this time. Forgive my information for being outdated."

"It is outdated in this time, but in your time, you said that Mr. Fitzwilliam Darcy, the last known master of that estate, had come into your county. What was that county?"

"Hertfordshire," I reported, "next to the village of Meryton."

"And you mentioned a Mr. Bingley, thinking he was connected to me? Do you know Mr. Bingley's name? His first name, I mean." He appeared eager for me to continue.

"Yes, it was Mr. Charles Bingley."

"And did he live in Hertfordshire?"

"Well, not yet, he has rented an estate that is three miles from where I live. He shall rent it at present but does not fully own it."

"And what is the name of this estate?" Again, he appeared to anticipate my answer.

"Netherfield Park."

❄

When I mentioned the name, Mr. Fitzwilliam Darcy bit his lip, then he moved away from me, and looked out of the window. After a moment of dreadfully awkward silence, he turned back to me.

"How do you know all this?"

"Because I was just told of it a couple of days ago."

"By whom?"

"By my father, for he had called on Mr. Bingley and learned of Mr. Darcy's accompanying his friend into the country."

"All right," he said with a groan, "this has gone far enough!"

"I beg your pardon?"

"What sort of dirty trick are you playing at here?" Mr. Darcy took a threatening step forward.

"I am up to no such thing! And how dare you accuse me of it? After all, this is my dream." I crossed my arms over the blanket that covered me.

"You know very well that you are not dreaming, so what are you? A trick, a busybody reporter that is still haunting my family during all this time?"

"What do you accuse me of? And this is a dream." Truly, I was beginning to worry a little.

"No, it is not. Now tell me what the bloody hell you are about?"

"I am up to nothing!" I cried, loudly enough for him to feel my impatience. "And it is most egregiously offensive that you insult me so."

49

"I am insulting you?" He inhaled sharply and his eyes turned venomous, to which I very quickly felt a natural impulse to despise him immediately. "How do you know about all this in regards to my family? Who have you been speaking with?"

My head began to ache again, and I pressed my fingers against my eyes. "I merely learned of this from my family who is wishing to meet Mr. Bingley at the assembly room, and Mr. Darcy is said to join him."

"Was, for as you know, he never made it there!" Mr. Darcy bellowed, to which I did not know what to make of anything he had said. What did he mean when he declared that Mr. Darcy had not made it there?

"Mr. Darcy!" Dr. Kennex cried. "Sir, she clearly is suffering from some sort of amnesia, that is all, and so, we merely have to be calm! Don't scream at her and be patient."

"Thank you," I said to Dr. Kennex, glaring at Mr. Darcy, who looked on me with a terrible scowl. Dr. Kennex, on the other hand, leaned forward and looked on me, his eyes sad for reasons I could not deduce. Then his shoulders hunched over, and I read in his countenance the reluctance of a man who was about to tell me a series of bad reports.

"Miss Elizabeth Bennet, unfortunately, I have some bad news for you. First, you are not dreaming. This is very much a reality. Everything that is happening, is truly happening. Also, England lost The War of 1812."

"I beg your pardon?" I could not believe him!

"Yes, and you lost it 204 years ago."

When he spoke this, my insides froze.

"And you are in Pennsylvania, in the United States of America, and the year, right now, is 2016."

# Chapter Six

## MY RELUCTANT HELPER

I was in the year 2016…

My brain could not sustain such a falsehood, and my immediate impulse was to deny it. However, the evidence before my very eyes could not be dismissed. Also, with the freshness of every action, with all appearing as authentic and real, I was beginning to no longer deny the possibility that the impossible had occurred.

After I appeared to be most disturbed by this, I requested a moment alone. Mr. Darcy, who was eyeing me uneasily, did not wish to relinquish his place in the room, but Dr. Kennex insisted. Both men left the room, with Mr. Darcy giving me a fleeting look, and then I was able to enjoy the peace that came with solitude.

Thank goodness he had left, for I could not concentrate with his gaze upon me—indeed, he seemed to be quite talented at making people uneasy.

When alone, I lay back, and found myself—to my surprise—as being quite unable to cry on the matter. All I could deduce was that I must have been so much in shock that I could not access my feelings at all.

Also, I was quickly desirous of finding a way in which to recover from this problem.

I was, perhaps, in the year 2016. All chance of that being real was impossible, but here it was, so I must handle it. If I had gotten misplaced in time, then there was the chance that I was not alone. Perhaps my family had been strangely transported in time. I needed to return to Longbourn!

Yes, that was it. If I could only return to England, then to Hertfordshire, I had to believe that my home was still there. Yet how was I to get there? I was divided from my home country by an ocean.

It required means and money. Yet perhaps, if I were able to send an express letter there, at least I could assure them that I was alive and well. However, it would take days. And they would not know what had happened to me, or with any luck, they would be quite distracted by their own woes. They would be too afraid with their new surroundings and it would take time to adjust to it. However, once they established themselves and adjusted to these strange changes, they would wonder after me, and not know what had occurred. They would not even know how to start. I needed to speak with them.

Or what if they were scattered, like I was? What if they had fallen —through time—and had woken up to find themselves so far from Longbourn, and away from each other? How horrible it would be for them to be separated from each other with no hope.

But dear me! I was truly adjusting to the possibility that this all could be real.

Yet it could not be.

And yet…it felt so. Indeed, it truly did feel so.

So could it be…

Upon my word, how quickly the mind can adjust to possibilities and ideas. And the revelation was now beginning to upset me. Filled with fear and trepidation, it could all be real. Yet if it was, then that meant that there might very well be no Longbourn to return home to. The idea frightened me greatly, and it made my head ache further.

I closed my eyes, overwhelmed by the idea of it, and how greatly I desired to be home again, to be as things always were—yet the more I remained in that bed, the more my mind, strangely so, began to accept that all around me was no dream, no fabrication of any kind.

*I had fallen through time…*

However, once I had thought the idea aloud, I was immediately frightened by it. That thought, mingled with the headache that was becoming worse from everything else, and with no arsenic to assist me, I grew weary, and before I knew what I was about, I felt my eyes close once more.

⚜

Yet my nap had not been for long as when I woke, I heard hushed voices outside of my door. However it did not belong to Dr. Kennex, but to Mr. Darcy—and Dr. Hoover.

"Dr. Kennex informed me of her state of mind," she commented, "and do you know how long she has been asleep?"

"Only for a half an hour," Mr. Darcy replied. "She is determined to believe her story."

"Perhaps she believes it because she really thinks it's true. While the accident has confirmed no mental damage, and she already was under a delusion when I met her, there might be something else going wrong here. Perhaps she had a tragic history."

"Tragic? How?" Mr. Darcy's voice did not sound confident.

"Perhaps she was captured, held for years, and made to believe that she was in the 19$^{th}$ century."

Mr. Darcy laughed bitterly, and I didn't like the sound of it.

"I doubt that. What would be the point in capturing someone and lying to them for years?"

"Have you ever read a newspaper in your life? Surely you've noticed that there are some sickos in the world."

"She gave no hints of physical abuse, and she is quite outspoken."

"True, if she were abused in any way, her spirit would be more timid and broken. She must really believe that she was born in that time period. And there is another possibility."

"And what is that?"

I listened to their conversation intently.

"Her x-ray indicates no sign of mental deterioration, but perhaps there is something that we did not see or has gotten overlooked. Perhaps she is suffering from some mental breakdown, a result of some trauma, and only time can see to it. This is not selective amnesia. This is true identity misplacement."

"And you really can't tell what it is?" His tone held skepticism. "Bleeding hell, you're doctors here."

"Mr. Darcy," she said calmly, "As a doctor I'm used to insults and such, but I'm not on the clock now so keep your opinions to yourself. Tomorrow we'll give her a visit from psychiatric, but in the meantime, something else has to be addressed."

"And what is that?" He continued to sound peeved.

"You have a medical plan."

"Yes."

"She needs someone to cover her."

"What?"

The vehemence in his voice startled me.

"Sir, she is in here for saving a child from your car," Dr. Hoover stressed, sounding cynical. "Is this where you think just by bringing her in, you have helped her in every way that you can?"

There was a moment of silence.

"Well, I thought that I wouldn't need to—It is just that, no one has even told me who she is. And she clearly doesn't know who she is. She only thinks that she knows."

I was secretly aggravated at his tone and I wished that I could throttle him.

Until the thought had quite occurred to me.

I needed to return to Longbourn and find my family.

And I needed a way to do it.

And there was only one way to achieve it.

I needed Mr. Darcy.

🐾

Mr. Fitzwilliam Darcy was the best option. In this world, where I knew absolutely nothing, I needed to survive and have a means to return. Continuing to deny that this world was not real was wasting time. The only way to return to England was learning to adjust to all that was around me. Setting aside my refusals to accept this new reality, I had to give way to finding a way in which I could go about removing myself from this infernal world and return to my own.

Mr. Darcy was from England, and Dr. Hoover seemed to be helping me in a way to suit my best interests, therefore I decided to remain quiet and continue to listen.

"It's not about the money," Mr. Darcy continued, "I'm fine with paying for everything, but there's another problem."

"And what is that?"

"I'm paying for a woman who claims to be from the 19th century and who also claims to know my family history. This is preposterous."

"Does that mean that you won't help her?" the doctor queried.

"I promised that I would, but I would like to know who she is, for as of right now, she appears to be insane."

I ground my teeth, and I felt myself so terribly offended, liking Mr. Darcy less and less as he spoke. Indeed, I knew that my appearance here was hard to accept, that he naturally would doubt my credibility, but he did not have to be so insufferably rude about it.

"Be careful not to use such controversial words," Dr. Hoover stressed, "especially in this case. Her mind seems to be mostly intact, her sense is impeccable, she knows who she is, so there is something else at work here."

"Are you implying that I ought to believe this nonsense?"

"Not at all. Naturally I know that time travel is impossible, despite how often any of us have watched 'Back to the Future', but we have to entertain the fact that this is a truth to her."

"Has there been no way to find out who she is?"

"She had no identity on her, and she claims not to have any at all."

"Well, that's just great!" He groaned, exasperated. "No identification, no sense of reality, and she woke up spouting facts about my family. This is utterly ridiculous."

The doctor was immediately alert. "What did you say? She knew about your family?"

"Yes, but never mind that. You mentioned that you were going to have some psychiatrists visit her to interrogate her?"

"Yes."

There was a momentary pause before Mr. Darcy spoke again. I held my breath.

"This may appear intrusive, but is there any chance of you interrogating her in a fuller proof method?"

"Mr. Darcy, are you implying a lie detector test?"

"I see no harm in it."

"I shall insist on her being inspected, but such measures are extreme."

"Doctor, you have a deranged woman in that room who claims to be from 1812. How else will you get to the bottom of it?"

Enough was enough! Whether he was my only means to return to England or not, I was not going to remain there and be insulted.

"Are you both quite finished?" I declared.

⚜

There was a moment of silence again, and then Dr. Hoover and Mr. Darcy entered the room slowly. I smiled at Dr. Hoover; I gave Mr. Darcy an imperious nod.

"Dr. Hoover," I welcomed.

"Miss Bennet," she replied, "I am glad to see you looking better."

"I am and thank you for everything. I woke up nearly a moment ago and I merely wished to inform you of such before I began to overhear something that I knew would make me quite beside myself." Here I gave a quick and cutting look to Mr. Darcy before I turned back to her. "So, you all don't believe me."

"Well," she began, "I don't mean to imply…"

"I know myself to be telling the truth," I began, "but I can see, from your viewpoint, what you must be thinking and feeling."

I rubbed my hands together, and then continued.

"I know, for a fact, that yesterday, I was in Hertfordshire, England, in 1812. Then suddenly I fall in a stream, wake up, and I am here. This all does feel real, and I have no choice but to accept that it is such. But mark my words, I am of sound mind, body, and I know where the truths are, however extraordinary they may seem. And I stand by what I say. Now, you were both speaking of a certain test?"

"Yes," Mr. Darcy said, "a lie detector test."

"And I am to deduce, that this test, by its title, is to determine, somehow if someone is lying?"

"Yes," Dr. Hoover explained. "It's a machine that you hook up to a person to determine if they are telling truths or not."

"A machine does this?" I asked, dubious.

"Yes."

"Is it harmful?"

"No, not at all."

"Will it enhance my chances of being believed and therefore being released from any limitations of any kind? It shall keep me from any unwanted visits from an asylum?"

"It will," Dr. Hoover replied, "You might have to remain here for a little further in the psych ward, but it shall perhaps be the safest place for you."

"That is out of the question," I stated firmly. "I have to go back to England and find my family. They won't know what has happened to me."

With that, Mr. Darcy gave me a firm look, but I avoided his gaze.

"Miss Bennet," Dr. Hoover continued, "you swear that you have no identification."

"I know that my name is Elizabeth Isabella Bennet. And that is all."

"Then I have to also do something else. I have to inform the authorities, and by that, I mean police, and with your permission, they must come in and copy your fingerprints so that they can identify you."

"Identify me?"

"It's a method we have. We use ink to identify individuals in our system."

"You use ink?"

"Yes, we place ink on a person's hands, then we have you press a paper and run your fingerprint through our records, called Interpol."

"Well," I said with a sigh, "this doesn't sound particularly harmful. Very well, you may do it."

I looked to Mr. Fitzwilliam Darcy, who looked positively doubtful about everything that I was saying.

"Still don't believe me, I see?" I asked him boldly.

He was taken aback by my direct question, and he shrugged.

"Well—it is just very hard to take this all in."

"I know the feeling," I replied, stone-eyed. "And yet I am to understand that you shall cover all my medical expenses?"

"I am."

"Then I thank you for that, for if this all be real, I am quite alone now and very afraid."

When I admitted this, Mr. Darcy's eyes softened for a moment and he looked entirely at a loss. Seeing his momentary vulnerability, I leaned forward, despite the pain that it caused.

"You do not believe me, I can see it in your eyes. But believe me, sir, all I want to do is get home. I am quite at a loss to explain what has occurred to me, but I am very much in a hurry to recover, and then to be removed from you as a burden. Yet I am lost now, and I wish to get back to my family. So, if this 'lie detector' instrument shall quicken your belief in my veracity, then so be it. Then afterwards, I shall need to recover, and…"

"And what?" he whispered.

"Well," I said with a sigh, a little frightened at my prospects, "I am a stranger here, in a strange land, unaware of how I got here or how to find my family and return home. Mr. Darcy, what you are witnessing now is a woman who is so terribly frightened, and unaware of what to do next. Therefore, thank you for assisting me, but the last thing I need for you to do right now is to assume that I am insane, or any other such offensive word that you put to it."

Mr. Darcy bit his lip, then he walked over to the window and looked out of it. I looked toward Dr. Hoover for an explanation, but she shrugged her shoulders, unaware of how to translate his behavior. At first, there was a bit of a silence.

"Mr. Darcy," I said, "forgive me for sounding impatient, but is there something out of the window that is better than I, sir?"

My snapping reply drew his attention and he turned back to me at last. I knew my remark to be harsh, but it was all that I could think about to draw his mind back to our conversation.

"I see that I have your attention," I observed.

"You do, and you do it most directly."

"Yes, I do. Perhaps it is because I am in pain, or because my fear has led to me having nothing to lose. But Mr. Darcy, I…"

"What is it?"

"It is nothing."

"But it is something. Go on then, spit it out. If you want me to apologize for what I did to you, then I really am sorry. I did all in my power to stop my car, and I feel much regret for hurting you. You must believe it, so if my—manner, has led you to believe that I don't care about what I did—"

"That was not what I was about to say."

"Then what were you about to say?" he hissed, and I immediately grew irate, my temper beginning to flare. Who was he to be so insufferable as to act this way? The hateful man!

"Mr. Darcy!" Doctor Hoover reprimanded.

"Mr. Darcy indeed," I hissed in return, and Mr. Darcy opened his mouth, then closed it again.

"I'm sorry." The words rushed out and then he calmed his voice. "It is only that—Miss Elizabeth Bennet, I hit you with my car. And while I have much sympathy for your situation, and I feel bad for what I did, but truth is, I feel bad for myself too."

"For yourself, sir?" I asked, bitter. The worthless man cared for himself in that moment, and not me.

"Imagine undergoing the frightening experience of hitting an innocent woman with your car, ma'am," he explained. "You are scared, yet so am I. And, as you can see by how I am behaving, there is no manual for how to deal with this."

When I looked on him, I felt a mixture of pity and disgust. I understood his feelings, very well did I comprehend them, but the fact remained that he cared for his own feelings and not mine. It didn't matter who I was, but he cared about his conscience, and no more. Yet I was still in the hospital bed, and therefore my pity was mostly still reserved for myself.

"I desire to take this test as soon as may be, and I shall also allow you to attempt to identify me, if that shall help remedy all the confusion and—"

Suddenly I heard the sound of the clock again, and I was quite overjoyed by it. Forgetting about the pain, I leaned forward and prepared myself.

"I'm waking up!"

☙❧

I closed my eyes, prepared, and I began to sink into my mind—and I felt myself as I was about to slip away. Mr. Darcy began to speak, but I paid no heed, and instead felt the bed beneath me slipping away, and his voice growing quite distant.

How delightful! I was now about to escape this dream, and I felt such comfort at the idea.

And then I smelled the familiar scent: the smell of the stream. I knew it very well, and I waited to feel my whole body immersed in the water. In fact, I felt my skin beginning to moisten, as if I had been submerged, and I was sufficiently prepared and ready to return to the world being right, and the sound of the clock grew louder and louder, therefore all was to be well.

Until I felt a touch on my arm.

A strong touch.

As it took hold of me, the smell of the stream began to slip away, water felt as if it was falling away from me and the sound of the clock began to grow faint.

Tick, tock, tick, tock, tick...tick...

Then nothing. The clock had all but faded, and all that was left for me to feel was the touch on my arm.

I opened my eyes and saw that the hand that was holding my forearm was Mr. Darcy himself. I may have had no proof of it, but I felt it within me, as sure as if there could be no other truth.

"You kept me from returning home!"

"Pardon?" He released my arm. "I thought you were passing out."

"I heard the sounds of the clocks," I cried.

"What clocks?" Dr. Hoover asked, then she looked me up and down, her expression one of puzzlement. "And you are practically drenched."

Indeed, I felt damp all over. "The clocks that I heard before I woke up in this world, in this time! And the clocks…it was clear that I was going to be returning home." I turned to Mr. Darcy, heartbroken. It was he that had kept me from returning. It was he that had made me unable to wake up from this dream. "Until you touched me. You're what is anchoring me down here!"

As if I had stricken him across his face, Mr. Darcy recoiled, and he clearly was horrified at my declaration. Now he would clearly think that I was mad, but Dr. Hoover came forward to inspect me.

"This is not sweat," she said, running her hand over my face, "for you were not warm a moment ago, and perspiration cannot form so quickly. She is soaking wet."

"I was in water," I announced. "Before I had woken up in this time period, I was walking in a stream, wading, and then something sucked me down, then I woke in the river. I was returning to that stream, I swear it. I know that it sounds strange, but I promise that I am not mad." I looked at Mr. Darcy once more, heartbroken. "I was ever so close to returning. So close to returning home."

"You didn't leave this bed," he replied. "Miss Bennet, you are being ridiculous."

"Mr. Darcy, please," Dr. Hoover interrupted.

"Forgive me," he replied. "I forget that you are still sick."

"And now I am angry." I began to weep. "Now I am so terribly frightened."

My look of sadness overwhelmed him, and he stepped away from me.

"Please," he continued, "I shall pay for your medical bills and I suppose, since this is my fault, I will make sure that you receive all the help that you need. I know we've got a large spot of bother, but I can tell you, this hospital is alright with its psychiatric program. I hope that you'll get better."

"You still believe me to be mad." I sighed, looking at him. "But, sir, I can assure you that I am not."

He looked firmly into my eyes while I looked on him with proud determination. I urged him to see that I was not insane, but I knew very well that I may have appeared so, and it broke my heart. This was no good, no good at all.

Yet I still needed him tremendously, for he might have thwarted me at the moment, but there still was a chance that he was my only means to return to England.

"Look at me," I urged, turning to Dr. Hoover. "You see it with your own eyes. I could not have perspired in this way so quickly." I touched my wet curls. "Even my hair is very wet. What other excuse could you find to counter my argument?"

The doctor looked at me, frightened, undecided whether to agree with me or not. She saw the logic of my statement but was scared to witness it clearly. Therefore, I had to continue on.

"Test me tomorrow," I said, "and hopefully that shall prove me right in the end."

# Chapter Seven

## THE COINCIDENCE

T hat night, one of the staff members showed me what a 'television' was, and then handed me the thing controlling it, which was called a 'remote control'. When I saw it, I did not know how to reply, for I was quite astounded at the concept behind it all. She turned to a channel that she said she enjoyed called AMC—while I want to believe that it stood for American Movies Classics, I could be in error.

She recommended a show on it called 'The Night Manager', and I can only assume that she thought it would make me feel comfortable, for many of the characters were British, but it was not of my time. I watched it anyway, not understanding half of what was being referenced, yet it was a masterpiece still, and it was all a marvel nevertheless!

A play! In a box! The entire show was captivating because of it. Though there was violence, I found myself quickly growing accustomed to it, because the nurse assured me that it was all just actors; after all, if I could read and watch Shakespeare, then who was I to be squeamish? 'Othello' followed the narrative of a villain who would result in killing his own wife.

When the show ended, I did my best to work the 'remote' and

found myself making a few mistakes where I increased the volume, pressed menu a couple of times by accident, and then eventually I stumbled on a channel called ABC, where it was playing a comedy of sorts that was on late night marathon called 'Modern Family'.

Now that one I was able to comprehend much, but as with the television, there were many devices on it that I could never imagine that I had dreamed up. Two episodes in and I still could not fully deduce what an 'iPad' necessarily was or could do.

Yet I could not sleep. For the television was a part of my imagination that amazed me, and I felt as if I wished to consume all that I had seen.

Then, when the television show ended, and some sort of advertisement played about some cleaning fluid called 'Tide', there was a man in it who reminded me of Mr. Darcy, and my mind turned back to him.

Why did my mind focus on him so much? What sort of character study was I forming in my subconscious that I made him the center of my dreams? I had never even met the real Mr. Darcy yet. And while a part of me believed that this might be some sort of alternate reality, the sound of the clocks and my near chance of returning home indicated that it still could all be unreal.

I almost had made it!

If only he had not touched me.

Yet, why was that so? By touching me, he anchored me to this time and place, as if he was a great weight. Yet that was highly improbable —but what was not near impossible in this instance? Everything indeed was most extraordinary, therefore, since impossible things were happening so very often at the moment, it therefore was likely that the only reason that I had remained was because Mr. Darcy had in fact held me there by grabbing me.

Yet what could that mean?

Indeed, all the puzzling questions were hurting my head and I was deeply unsettled. I knew not why I was not more afraid, yet I suppose it was because while I was lost, I still felt safe. According to them, the war I worried over had been over for centuries, so I would not be arrested, and they were kind enough to care for me. They did not need to, but they did nonetheless.

"Well, Lizzy," I said to myself, "I suppose, if there was one place that I would get lost in, this was the best of times, and still it is the scariest of times."

I was distracted when the show Modern Family came back on, and then I continued to watch it, hoping this 'marathon' would last till the early morning.

❃

The next day, I was visited by a psychiatric team of three individuals, but Dr. Kennex was there to oversee them. With speed they also placed a 'lie detector test' on me, that scared me initially, but when I saw that it was not harmful, I calmed down.

I was acquainted with the fact that the test was not a usual thing that they possessed at the hospital, so there was a police official there to oversee the procedure, for it was taken from some authority site called 'a police precinct'.

The police woman attached the machine to me, and then I apologized for any offense I gave for being surprised that she was a female. She readily softened, and we proceeded to get the process underway.

Dr. Kennex asked me a series of questions about where I came from, my upbringing, and how I got to where I was then. From my family history, to when I woke up in the Delaware River, I reported all, and when I finished, it was announced to me that I had passed the test.

They knew that I lied about nothing.

❃

The police woman also placed ink on my fingers and took down my prints, and I recalled that that was the step that would be used for them attempting to identify me. I agreed to this scheme, because I loved the idea of being about to discover how I was listed in their strange system. If my existence was proved, then all the better, and all the more chances that I would be able to find my family.

Eventually, I was left alone once more, and I was given my dinner, which was actually quite enjoyable of a meal, when the nurse allowed me to watch the television once more.

There I sat, eating while this time watching the television show called 'Empire'—when my mind turned toward Jane.

She would be so worried over me. And Mary, Kitty, and perhaps even Lydia was weeping, wondering what had happened. And my father, oh dear me! I left with no explanation.

I thus became forlorn over the idea that I was causing them grief, and I rubbed my eyes, wiping away the emotion, when I felt eyes upon me.

This sensation was followed by a knock, and I looked up, toward the door of my hospital bedroom. There, with a rose in his hand, stood Mr. Darcy.

☙❧

"Is that for me?" I asked softly.

"Yes," he said, approaching me. "I suppose, that I hoped that you like roses."

"It is lovely."

He handed me the flower, I took it and smelled it.

"Peach roses are always a beauty," I said, "and it smells quite nice." Unlike the flower in the vase at my bedside.

"I am glad that you like it."

Mr. Darcy was looking at me quite strongly, and I sensed that there was something else under his expression, so I assumed it was the test.

"They tested me today," I reported.

"Yes," Mr. Darcy said, rubbing his hands together and fidgeting. "I heard. They say that you passed the test."

"I did. I lied about nothing."

"Yes, there is the chance that you were telling the truth."

"You doubt me still?" I gasped, "and you—"

Mr. Darcy was looking somewhat bewildered. Indeed, there was a great unease to him as he clearly couldn't stand still. Filled with nervous energy, he moved away from me and then sat down in a seat against the wall—just staring at me.

"Mr. Darcy…"

"It's not that I doubted you necessarily," he elaborated, "it is just, I have learned that there is a defect to the test."

"A defect?" I groaned, "What are you implying, sir? For this morning I was attached to a machine that I thought could kill me, and the sight of it still overwhelms me, so I don't need any more surprises."

"Sometimes a lie detector can be inaccurate."

"And how is that?"

"If a person can believe that they lived in 1812, even if they didn't, they can pass the test. Due to their mind's ability to trick itself."

"I do not pretend to be ignorant of what you are referring to, but I resent it. Do I look like the sort of person that could deceive anyone, let alone that blasted machine? Oh, forgive my words, I know I was being vulgar just now."

"Can you please just…" He sighed, wringing his hands, and then he collapsed into the chair, somewhat bewildered. As he sat there, I didn't know that it was possible to feel pity for him, but in that moment, I did.

I suppose, in his countenance, I saw a heaviness, and he just didn't know what to make of me, as I didn't know what to make of him. Neither of us knew what to do at present, but we seemed to quickly become an unwanted burden to each other.

Until I remembered my family, and how I desperately needed to get back to them.

I needed Mr. Darcy on my side, and I had to begin to find a way to do so.

"I am causing you grief and confusion," I began. "I can see that, and I regret being the means behind your woes. For that, I am sorry. But for the rest, I am guiltless."

"Yes, thank you. And again," he said, raising his face to mine; his eyes were heavy, "I am sorry for how we have met."

"Well, now." I gave him a weak smile. "it's nice to hear an apology again. You have done it before, but that one was well done."

"Thank you."

He leaned back in his chair and his eyes rested on me. It unnerved me slightly, for I did not know what to make of him, and it was hard to bear the sight of him when his eyes were fiercely upon me.

"Sir, forgive me, but it is a little rude to stare."

"Right, sorry about that," he said, looking down at the ground. "Miss Bennet, yesterday, you mentioned bells."

"Yes, the bells of a—"

"Clock."

"Yes, it was such."

"And you heard it before you claimed to have woken up in the river, and when you were sitting on the bed."

"Yes, I heard it as I was speaking with you."

"What— what was the sound like?"

"Well," I began, confused at why he needed detail about something so very simple, "it was like the bells on any grandfather clock. The sound it can make when it reaches the hour, but this time, the sound was quite loud. It kept going on and on, getting louder and louder, and then I felt as if I was, well I cannot describe the sensation, but it felt as if I was being—"

"Pulled down?" he suggested, warily.

"Yes," I concurred, but I was also observant, and I noted how his suggestion was so close to what I had undergone. How could he have understood the experience? Unless… "I felt as if I was being pulled down, and then—dear me, I cannot find the words to explain the next part."

"Then it felt as if you were being hurled through water?" he proposed, and that was enough.

"Yes," I said, looking boldly at him, and my expression read clear as day: you know what I am undergoing now! You know it, indeed. When Mr. Darcy saw this, he looked down at his hands that rested on his lap. "Yes, that is precisely as it was. You describe my experiences quite accurately, sir. Too accurately."

He wouldn't meet my gaze. "I noticed how you woke up wet the other day."

I leaned toward him. "But that is not how you spoke of it. No, you spoke with too much comprehension of the matter, as if you had experienced this all firsthand. Mr. Darcy, please, look at me, sir. I am a creature to be pitied, and you seem to know what I have undergone. How would you know that? Sir, do you know how I have come to be here? Do you have any knowledge about my abduction?"

"Miss Bennet, I swear, I don't know anything. I don't know how you got here, or if I even fully believe you yet."

"Then how did you understand what I had undergone when being cast out in your time, sir?"

"Because I heard the clock."

❈

When Mr. Darcy spoke this, I could not believe my ears, so I repeated his acknowledgement.

"The clock?"

"I heard it," he confessed.

I noticed he was shaking as he leaned toward me.

"Yes. I was in my hotel room last night and I heard the sound of a clock out of nowhere."

"And there are no clocks in your hotel room at all?"

"No, there are not. Well, there are only electronic ones. But they don't make any sound."

"Strange thing, indeed," I mused, tucking a wayward curl behind my ear. "Not having a real clock."

"It is customary to not always have them."

"Then how may the friendly visitor and guest tell the time?"

Mr. Darcy took out something from his hand, touched it and then showed me the time from the object.

"Well," I said, not so much impressed as I was bewildered, "that is a very interesting...time piece."

"It's called a cell phone."

"A cell phone?"

"It means cellular phone. We call and talk to people on it."

"What?" One new strange contraption after another. How was I to take it all in? "That is just...what?"

"Yes," he said, appearing to stop a smile. "I still wonder if I can believe you, but this is quite comical."

"Does it look like I am pretending?" I took his appliance from him without even bothering to ask for it first.

"Hey!"

"Forgive me, but I am merely intrigued is all. What are all these other buttons for?"

Mr. Darcy took it back from me quickly.

"They are icons. For example, this one here I can click and view my calendar, and then this one is my address book where I can find a phone number that I wish to call. And this one over here is where I click if I want to look up something on the internet."

I was amazed as he showed me this.

"But, what precisely is an *internet*?"

Mr. Darcy bit his lip and then he put his phone away.

"It is this, well, it's like a technological encyclopedia where you can look up anything you want and—I'm bloody terrible at explaining this."

"You know, you really don't need to swear."

"No need to swear?" he scoffed. "I'm in a hospital room explaining the internet to a woman who has claimed to travel through time because I heard some bells. I have every wanking reason to be swearing, don't you think?"

"Wait, you said you heard bells?"

When I repeated his accidental confession, Mr. Darcy blinked and then he looked down at the ground. He had not meant to give that away, but he had, and there was no going back.

"That is why you have come here." I was overjoyed that he had no choice now but to see that I was not being deceptive. "And why you are asking me all these questions as well as empathizing with what I am going through. In fact, it's not empathy, is it? It's shared experience. You heard the bells too? And you woke up covered in water?"

"I was probably overheated," he excused, "and it could have been a daydream. I daydream a lot."

"Everyone daydreams often," I rushed out, eager to get him past his state of denial. "Therefore that is no excuse at all. Mr. Darcy, please do not deny it, for your acceptance of the matter is what shall help us be able to come to an understanding."

"An understanding?"

"Yes, I need you to believe me. When you heard the clock, it grew louder and louder, and then you felt as if you were being pulled down, through many layers of earth and water, and then was about to be pushed away somewhere else. Fear gripped you, and then you knew even beforehand that you were being pushed to some place. You were being transported—and it was through water."

Mr. Darcy turned away from me and went to the window.

"I must be losing my mind," he murmured.

"Oh, thank you for that analysis," I replied, annoyed, "for if you are going insane, then that means I am so, and I do not like that notion."

"Are you bleeding kidding?" He wielded on me with a passion. "The idea of time travel. It's all mental!"

"Mental?"

"It means to go insane."

"Ah...mental. When one is saying that one is losing one's mind, we ought to say that we are going mental?"

"Yes."

"Ah."

"Now don't distract me," he rushed on, "for listen to yourself. You are suggesting that you were transported through time, and that I almost was, and you do not know how at all."

"Do I look like the sort of person to understand an equation that could lead to me comprehending time and the universe, sir? I wish I could give you an answer, but I cannot. But it cannot be denied. Time is...being crazy."

"Be careful, for you sound like the 'Doctor'." He paced back and forth.

"Which one, Dr. Hoover or Dr. Kennex?"

"No, sorry, right. When I meant the Doctor, I meant the TV show."

"TV show? On that?" I asked, pointing to the television.

"Yes, it's a show we have nowadays about time travel. It's called 'Doctor Who'."

"You have a television series about time travel?" This was exciting news to me.

"Oh, there are many movies, books, and shows about time travel. For example, there is 'Back to the Future', '2001, A Space Odyssey', 'Star Trek', 'The Terminator', 'Edge of Tomorrow' a bit, 'Legends of Tomorrow', the list is endless."

Though the names meant nothing to me, my interest was peaked. "So research has already been done on this concept?"

"Well, only in fiction and entertainment, and not actual reality. There is no equation, as you put it, or method through which time travel has ever been made possible."

"But the idea has been explored through these mediums. Time has been considered to be something you can travel through?"

"Only in the fictitious sense," Mr. Darcy kept on pointing out, "and not in the literal or realistic sense."

While this was not a very promising start, it was better than nothing, so I had to go from there and convince Mr. Darcy, to the best of my ability, that I was in earnest.

"Mr. Darcy, may I call you Fitzwilliam?"

"Please call me Fitz, for indeed, I hate my full name."

"And I can see why." I smiled gently, and then I grew serious, "Fitz, I promise you I am not lying. The test, however it works, has also confirmed this. I am not lying to you now, and I need you to believe me. I know I cannot ask for help from you, but if you would be willing to do so, then I would be grateful. Yet now, I first need simply for you to have faith in me. Fitz, it can be only this. I traveled through time. And I'm further from home than I thought."

⚜

"And you almost traveled through time yourself," I corroborated.

"Impossible."

"That's what happened, sir."

"I was just hallucinating."

"I thought I was dreaming before, and look what happened? I know denial is easier. For if it were so, then that would mean that everything I have just undergone is not actually happening. That I am not separated from England by an entire ocean—that I am not separated from my family, and Longbourn, by over two hundred years.

"For if this is all true, then my family, if they haven't travelled forward in time with me, are dead now, have been for over a century, and I am alone in this world."

I thought again of my loving family and my heart twisted in my chest. "If that is so, then take your fears, your woes, and magnify them by a hundred. That is what I am undergoing now.

I choked back tears. "I am so terrified, Fitz. So utterly terrified, and I have no idea what to do," I confessed, nearly weeping. "Therefore, at least let me have the pleasure of your belief in me, and not let pride in what we both know as truths prejudice you against the fact that is now presented to us. Fitz, please..."

His strong and bold countenance was still, and his expression was mixed between a scowl and one of confusion.

"I cannot believe this."

"You can," I urged.

"I don't...I don't want to believe this."

"But you must."

There was a pause for a moment, as we were both quite silent.

"You really are not lying to me," he voiced, more to himself than to me.

"Yes," I confirmed.

"I don't wish to believe this."

"But you believe it all the same. We have undergone the same situation. Except whatever happened was successful with me, but what happened with you was not."

"And why would that be?" His eyebrows drooped as they showed signs of resignation.

"I don't know," I whispered. "I am entirely at a loss. Um, but then..."

"What?"

"In that movie you said before, the uh, Doctor Who show?"

"Yes," he said, sighing, and then he chuckled once. "Forgive me, but you mention it like you are speaking another language."

I ignored his tone. "How does time travel work in that story?"

"He has a time machine that looks like a giant phone box."

"Oh." I frowned, disappointed. "Well, that doesn't seem like it could help us at all."

"No, perhaps it does not."

"And with the other one, 'Back to the Future', what happened there?"

"Oh, a character created a car that could travel through time."

"Oh, those carriage things. Cars."

"Yup."

"Does that mean yes?"

"Yes, it does."

"Right. So one has a phone box and the other has a car. I used neither of those things. There was no contraption used—there was only the sound of the clock."

"And the sensation of being drenched in water," Fitz added.

"Yes, that as well." I smiled up at him. "Then you believe me?"

He gave me a wry sort of smile. "I still wish that I was going mental instead."

"Well, if you are mental, it's not because of what has just occurred here."

"Oh, thanks mate!" he scoffed.

"Forgive me, I was merely wishing to offer a joke. Is it too soon into our acquaintance for me to do so?"

With a sigh, he sat down. "You were trying to make the moment lighter."

"It helps me to cope with all that I am experiencing."

"I just realized something."

"Yes?"

"I never told you that I am sorry for the loss of your family. If this all is real, then I truly am sorry."

"Thank you," I replied heavily, feeling the weight at last in full "Yet in truth, I cannot think of that fully just now."

"You cannot?"

"No, I must believe that they are alive somehow and that I can get back to them. I need to believe that." I was fervent in my belief.

"I can well understand that."

We were interrupted when something rang in his pocket. Fitz looked at the cell phone, offered his excuses, raised it to his ear and began to speak into it.

I was once again mesmerized and perplexed. Another new contraption for me to understand!

For a time, I tried not to listen, but then the conversation turned toward me, and Mr. Darcy told the other person that he was in Philadelphia, where he was detained due to an accident. Eventually, the call ended with him saying, 'I love you' to the speaker and then the conversation ended.

I gave him a puzzled look. "So, you really can speak to someone through that?"

He frowned and glanced at the cell phone in his hand and then explained the function to me. I did not fully understand, but I said, "They must be worried about you. I don't mean to be intrusive, but who was that? Your mother or sister?"

"No, it is my fiancée."

"Your fiancée? Oh, are you to be married, sir?"

"We've been engaged for over a year now. Her name is Caroline Bingley."

# Chapter Eight

## WHAT HAPPENS NOW?

"Oh." There was a change in my attitude toward Fitz. "You are to be soon married."

"Yes, I am."

"And when this is supposed to be a happy moment for you, instead this has happened. And now you've got me on your woes."

"I suppose that it has been a little puzzling to me, but you don't need to worry about keeping me away from things. Getting married is not so much between two people as it is between two hundred."

"What do you mean?" I fussed with my hair, knowing I must look a mess.

"Well, I do not really find myself spending time assisting anyone when it comes to the wedding plans," he replied softly, and it appeared, for a moment, that all his strength seemed to leave him. If I had not known any better, he appeared to be tired at the moment.

"My fiancée takes care of all that herself, along with the other women in her family. And we men find it best to remain clear of them when they go about it."

"Well, I suppose that of course is the way it always is. The women prepare everything, and it is the groom's duty to simply...present himself on the day. Sober and sound of mind are all that is required of him." I chuckled to lighten the mood. "Yet if I may be so bold, for a man who claims that getting married is of no inconvenience to himself, you do appear tired."

Fitz looked at me and then looked away, but not before I could discern a certain something in his eyes. If I was not mistaken, it was a sort of pain. He was troubled over something or confused. And I knew that it was me quite well.

"And I'm the reason that you are tired," I magnified.

"No, it's not that."

"Yes, it is, and I am sorry over it. Really, I am. I did not intend any of this, I can assure you."

He raked his fingers through his dark brown hair. "I know."

For a time, we sat there in silence, until I realized something.

"Wait, you said her name is Caroline Bingley?"

"Yes."

I covered my mouth with my hand, instantly alarmed. "You are marrying Mr. Bingley's sister?"

⚜

"But how can that be?" I asked, surprised. "For we were told only a brief time ago that Mr. Bingley's sisters were traveling with him into Hertfordshire. Then again, so were you."

"First, my fiancée has no brother. She is the oldest of her sisters. There are three of them in total."

"Miss Bingley has no brother?"

"No, she does not. And secondly, you must not talk as if I am the same Mr. Darcy."

"Yes." I laughed bitterly. "I am pulled out of time and place, pushed into a distant future of my time while you are getting married to a Bingley woman, and the most absurd thing that I can do is mention a split infinity."

"A split infinity?"

"Yes, where one thing is happening in one area, and then the same thing is happening in another."

"That's what you think this is," he furthered, drawing his chair

77

close to my bed. "You think that you were brought here, to me, and there is another Mr. Darcy waiting for you in Hertfordshire still?"

I was becoming quite agitated. "I do not know about that at all, I was merely suggesting—and Mr. Darcy and I are not acquainted at all. Therefore, he is not my Mr. Darcy, as you called him."

"And you really have not met him?"

"No, I have not. We were expecting to."

"Right." He leaned back, looking quite disappointed. "I was hoping that you could tell me something."

"Such as? Like how he disappeared?"

"Yes," he replied, then he rubbed his nose and stood up. "Well, I best be off."

"You're upset with me for not knowing more," I voiced, and he turned to me with consideration.

"I had hoped…I had…never mind, I should let you rest now."

"Is this where I never see you again?"

Mr. Darcy turned, looked at me, and his jaw turned firm.

"I'll see you tomorrow."

"Thank you. For indeed, I feel so very alone."

"I know the feeling."

"And again, I am sorry that I am ruining your most happy moment. Yet I trust that Miss Bingley shall forgive me."

"Yeah, she will, I suppose."

With that, he left.

◈

And with his departure, thus came the arrival of my apprehensions and worries. Despite our turbulent past, his was the last face that my face had seen before I had passed out on the road. He was the only face that I kept seeing every time that I would wake up. Therefore, if I never were to see him again, it would be altogether strange.

Yet there was hope. He now heard the bells, and therefore, we were both connected. We had a shared experience.

And a name, for Caroline was a Bingley.

That could be no coincidence. Perhaps there was something about her that could also assist us both. Her family was the main link that was there, for there was a Mr. Bingley in my history and there she was in this one. Perhaps, when the matter was explained, she would help us, and that was a comforting thought.

I turned on the television again and watched a show called 'Law and Order', and proceeded to understand the majority of it, but still not fully comprehending.

Two days later I woke up from a nap to the sound of voices. My spirits increased when I heard that it was Mr. Darcy's voice responding to Dr. Kennex.

"So, you called me down here to tell me this?" Mr. Darcy asked, sounding slightly vexed.

"Yes, for I thought it might be better to tell you in person rather than over the phone."

"Why not a phone call, then?"

"Because I am going to need to know, after this, if you shall help her at all."

"And what do you mean?"

I kept quite still and continued to listen.

"What I mean is that the database at the police station has concluded, with no firm results."

"No results?"

"We assumed we would have her identity soon, yet we don't. The data has come back, and it is inconclusive."

"You found nothing?"

"Nothing at all. She has no record, no identity at all, and therefore we have no way of telling you who she is."

"Bloody hell," Mr. Darcy spat. It sounded like he had covered his mouth. "I can't believe it."

"Yes, but therein lies another matter."

"What?"

"Mr. Darcy, I know very well that she speaks of time travel and supernatural elements, but she appears and acts sane. However, between her lack of an identity mingled with her declarations that she comes from another time, it shall potentially be recommended that she would be sent to a…psychiatric hospital. She shall be admitted into…"

"She shall practically be sent to an asylum," Mr. Darcy summed up.

"Precisely."

My ears pricked up. A psychiatric hospital?

"Well, I can very well believe that would be the logical outcome."

"Is that where you believe that she should be placed?"

There was a silence, where I could imagine that Mr. Darcy was the one who was hesitant to speak for a time.

"Well, sir, is it? I know what she says sounds impossible, but it could come from the mind of someone who is merely confused."

"Whether she is confused or not, she is one hundred percent sane."

"You see this as well."

"Yes, I do. She very much is not mad."

Relief swept through me.

"And," continued the doctor, "I know that your life is anything but normal right now, but you will be returning to England soon, and with her being from there—well, I have seen this before. The smallest thing could jog her memory back into place. One familiar sight in London, walking on a street where she lived or walked down once, that might be it. And, forgive me for noticing, but I understand that money is not a priority with you, for your family is—"

"Filthy rich," Fitz interjected. "Yes, we bloody well are, now excuse me while I sigh."

"Sigh away. Again, I know that this is the last thing that you need."

"But I am responsible for her," Fitz concluded.

"Well, I did not mean to imply that and make you feel guilty."

"But it's so, isn't it?" he replied, sounding very introspective, as if he was speaking more to himself, pondering his own reflections than talking with the doctor. "I mean, you know, I hit her with my car. And this is my fault. Dear god, I never meant to hurt her."

"Of course you didn't."

I continued to listen with interest and enthusiasm.

"We humans have this annoying tendency to crash into each other, don't we?" Fitz chuckled bitterly. "Well, I don't know what I can do for her, but the least I can do is look after her and take her in for a time. You might be right, mate. To London is where she perhaps needs to be."

"You'll look after her?"

"I can, for a time."

My enthusiasm heightened.

"Well, I want to believe that she will be well under your care, but I shall have to demand that I check in with you every now and again, to make sure that she will be in a healthy environment and that she is not being mistreated. This is unorthodox, but I have the feeling that a psych ward is the last place she ought to be put. This is a risk, but I am depending on you."

"She doesn't have much of a choice, but if you're implying that I'm not trustworthy, then beggars can't be choosers, now can you?"

"Fitz, I didn't mean to…"

"I know you didn't. Sorry, I was mean just then, but it couldn't be helped. This whole situation is trying my patience. When she wakes up, you may break the news to her about it."

"You don't have to," I said at last, "for I'm awake, gentlemen."

৩ॐৎ

Once both men recovered from the surprise of learning that I had overheard everything, they came in and Doctor Kennex explained it to me. I agreed to the situation very quickly, for what other choice did I have? In fact, this was the best outcome that there ever could have been.

After Dr. Kennex settled everything, he left me alone with Fitz, who stood there awkwardly as I studied him.

"I know that this is hard for you to do," I confessed, and then I smiled gently. "And I know the trouble this is causing you, but really Fitz, thank you ever so much."

To show my adoration of his willingness to assist me and not leave me to the whim of chance, I held out my hand.

"Please, take hands with me, for I have no other way of showing you my gratitude."

He gave a sad chuckle, approached me and then embraced my hand in his own.

"You have quite saved my life," I noted. "I shall not forget that. And still, I promise you, that I shall do everything in my power to not impede on your time of happiness. With any luck, I shall be removed from your life even before the wedding."

"Don't worry, it'll be fine. I know this is the best thing, for you as well as me."

"For we have many questions, do we not?" I gave him a conspiratorial smile.

"Yes, we do, and I suppose that I have no choice but to go down this rabbit hole."

"Rabbit hole?"

"Oh, I use it as a metaphor right now. It is, well, it is…I'll just introduce you to the movie 'Alice in Wonderland' one day, and then it shall be explained."

"Sounds… spectacular."

"Yes, yes. Yes."

# Chapter Nine

## HOW AWKWARD A BEGINNING

Over the next couple of weeks, I was soon getting closer to being on the mend, and I did not see much of Mr. Darcy in that time. He informed me that he naturally had business to attend to and had to plan with his fiancée.

"But does she know of this situation?" I asked when he came to visit me two weeks before the doctors determined that I was allowed to come home. "I just wished to inquire if your fiancée fully comprehends that you are assisting me and coming to my aid, and that is all. Believe me, I have five sisters and I have seen what happens when miscommunication springs from jealousy."

"Why would my fiancée be jealous of you?" He was quite oblivious to what I had meant.

"No." I laughed. "That is not what I mean. You shall be taking me with you back to England, therefore naturally Miss Bingley would desire to know of it. Also, it can look opposite to what you intend—I do not wish for you to get into trouble all because of me."

He nodded, digesting this. "Yes, point taken. I had intended to do it in the right time, yet things have quite overwhelmed me."

"And you know a Miss Bingley." I drew in a sigh. "So that is familiar at least."

"Yes," he replied, unsure of how to respond.

"I know that I should not speak in such a way, for it causes you pain. So, if you could tell me, what part of London are you from?"

"Oh, I merely rent when in London," he replied, "but you already know about Pemberly in Derbyshire."

"Oh, yes, quite right."

"When I get married, I'll spend even less time there."

"Why would you? For I have heard of it being such a great estate."

"Too great of an estate. It's like a museum. And with all that space, there's not much to it, now is there?"

"Why?" I asked. "Are you lonely?"

Mr. Darcy looked at me sharply, and then looked down at his hands.

"I'm getting married soon."

"Yes, of course," I replied, not convinced with that response. "Forgive me, of course you are not lonely."

"You must simply understand the times," he added, leaning forward, and eyeing me in a most direct fashion that quite unnerved me. "You really do believe that you are not from this time, don't you? I mean, I thought you were just a little cream-crackered from exhaustion and also perhaps a little bonkers, or just lying for fun, but you're not.

"I can't deny that you are not mental, you seem sane enough really, and you don't have the ways or manners of a person playing at something, so you really must believe what you are having at. You really do believe that you are from a different time period."

"That much I know for a fact," I determined. "What I still am choosing to put faith in however, is if this world is real."

"This world?" He turned from the window, gave me a puzzled look and returned to the chair by my bed.

"Your world. You see, any moment now, I want to wake up, and I'm hoping that I shall. Therefore, the only thing I'm certain about, is that I am Elizabeth Bennet, of Longbourn, in Hertfordshire England, and it's you that I don't believe is real."

"You doubt me being the genuine article?"

"Yes, because I was simply apprehensive about meeting the real

Mr. Darcy, and so I believe that I created you in my mind, to show that."

"To show what?"

I pinched my cheek with my teeth, unwilling to respond, but I didn't need to at present, for instead Fitz walked toward me slowly, then he placed his hand around mine.

"Do I feel fake?" he asked. "Do I feel as if I'm not real?"

"One doesn't know one is in a dream when one is. Nothing ever feels artificial, and all feels solid," I explained, smoothing the blanket over my knees.

"I am real," he replied, "because, if I wasn't, then you should have woken up by now."

He hunkered close to me. "Think about it, you woke up in a river, rode a ferry boat, and then got hit by a car—also you've been here for weeks. How far do you think this dream would take you? I am real, Miss Bennet. It's you that makes me doubt reality. Now, you still did not answer me. Why would you need to dream me up to face me in reality?"

"Why are you running from living in Pemberly?" I asked him, out of curiosity while also hoping to distract him from continuing to inquire about something that I didn't wish to talk about. Luckily, to my benefit, it had worked quite well.

"First," he replied, his eyes hardening, "it is the way of the times. While some still live in large homes, most of us have adapted to change, and do not wish to maintain such grandeur, and always maintaining rooms that we don't even use. It's not very contemporary, now is it?"

"And what is contemporary?"

"Townhouses work the best. And all that aristocratic languor— well, it's just not my thing. Pemberly, it's just not me at all. It belongs to my family, but I don't need to live in a museum, and it makes me feel like I would be regarded as a museum-piece myself."

I glanced at the table beside me, where someone had placed a single flower in a vase. "I never would have viewed it that way."

"Well, since I have no choice but to believe you, when you see what London looks like now, you'll understand why I can't stay at Pemberly."

"Does London look anything like Philadelphia?"

"Yes and no. The setup of Philadelphia is different than London's but the cosmopolitan life is similar. If you like Philadelphia, then you most likely will like London. But London, well, London is—it's like the world in itself."

I took the vase from the table and sniffed it; unlike flowers at home, it had little aroma. As I replaced it, I said, "I always prefer the country as opposed to town."

"There are just so little amount of people out in the country."

"Yes, there is, but that never shackled me. I suppose, I'm harder to make bored." Although boredom certainly was high on my list at the moment.

"Why?"

"Because I enjoy observing others. I find it to be amusing."

"Amusing? Then, when you met me, you must not have had much to figure out, because I am very easy to comprehend," he announced.

I hid a smile. "I am not too certain about that. It does not follow that a deep, intricate character is more or less estimable than such a one as yours."

"I did not know before," he continued, "that you were a studier of character. It must be an amusing study."

"Yes, but intricate characters are the *most* amusing. They have at least that advantage."

He stood and returned to the window. I could hear a roaring overhead, I knew not what it was. "The country can in general not have many people for you to observe. In a country neighborhood you move in a very confined and unvarying society."

I studied his back, his shoulders, broad and handsome, the cut of his clothes unusual, certainly not something I was accustomed to. "But people themselves alter so much, that there is something new to be observed in them forever."

"But London would offer more chances to observe more people."

"But London has something that can hinder that, Fitz."

He turned and pinned me with a puzzling look. "And what would that be?"

"Noise." I laughed. "Too much noise."

"Then, I can't convince you. You don't like the city."

"Oh, I never said that. The city has its benefits, and I find it excessively diverting sometimes. I just enjoy the freedom of being able to…"

"To what?"

"To run about. To be free from prying eyes. To be without restraint sometimes."

"Well, then you shall be really happy."

"Why so?"

"Because London is like that now. You can run as much as you want in certain places, and be mad and manic in others, and all without being called mental."

"Go on," I said disbelievingly. "I know you are mocking me, sir."

"No, I'm bloody well not."

"Come then, that is going too far. How could I believe such things?"

"London has really changed since 1812, and of course it ought to be, for you have seen yourself what the passage of time can do."

"Yes," I said with a sigh, "perhaps I have. Then, you really believe me now?"

"Yes, I do. I pretty much have no choice in the matter, when you think about it."

"Whether you do or not, I am glad of it, for it helps a great deal," I admitted kindly. "Thank you. Your faith in me is a great comfort."

He smiled at me and then looked down at his hands that were folded on his lap.

❦

"And you mentioned a second reason for why you are almost never at Pemberly," I urged.

"Ah, yes. Ah, yeah. My work takes me there a lot."

"Your work?" I asked, confused. "But then—are you implying, sir, that you have a profession?"

"Yeah, naturally." He tilted his head and gave me a strange look.

"But what sort of profession?"

"Oh, my father founded an advertising agency, and therefore I inherited it."

"Then even your father worked?"

"Why do you sound so surprised by this?"

"It is just…you are a landed gentry. Therefore, it is not customary for landed gentry to be men of profession. Besides, are you not a gentleman?"

When I said this, his brow furrowed and then comprehension dawned over his face, and he understood.

"Oh, yes, now I get it. In Georgian England, landed gentry are not men who work, right? They all were fancy twats who stayed at home all day, doing nothing except talk about the many things that they thought about doing, but didn't."

"Do not sneer at our background," I replied, growing defensive, for my father was still regarded as being of landed gentry. While Mr. Darcy's description was accurate mostly, I still was not willing to agree to his generalization.

"You may look after your estate with care, cultivate it, and also profit by having tenants on your estate that you oversee."

"Ah, to be chained to dirt." He shook his fine head. "I find that I'm not that crazy about that idea."

"You truly do sneer at the idea of the country?"

"I don't hate the country, it's just that well, my heart is here—in a city."

"Well, I am not averse to other perspectives. Besides, being in town can be diverting, so I can well comprehend, as I had spoken."

However, while I very well understood his mindset, I still felt as if there was more that he was not letting on. Yet it was not in my way or manner—or even right—to pry into his internal feelings, for if I did, he would soon feel it correct to attempt to delve into mine. And I truly was not ready for him to delve at present—if ever.

Fitz—what are you? A philosophical question, I know, but still, if it was all a dream, then why did my mind choose him? Yet if he was real, and I had traveled in time, then why did time bring me into his life?

Or perhaps I was looking for parallels where there was none.

Perhaps it was all merely circumstances.

# Chapter Ten

## MY NEW KEEPER

Eventually I was released from the hospital and was placed into Fitz's care. Before leaving, Dr. Hoover visited me. She was quite kind, and I worried that I would very much never see her again. For once leaving, soon with any luck, I would return to England, and she had been most cordial.

When I finally parted from her, I was pulled along in a thing called a wheelchair, and then rolled out to Mr. Darcy's car. When he pulled up, I was impressed by the way the car looked, for it was quite breathtaking.

"My goodness," I gasped when I beheld it, "you actually ride this sort of thing?"

"Why shouldn't I?"

"Sorry, it is just so so…cool."

Mr. Darcy blinked. "Did you just say the word 'cool'?" He smirked.

"Yes, well, I might've overheard Dr. Kennex say that when he was speaking to one of the nurses about a show called 'Game of Thrones', and at first, I thought that he meant that it was cold, but I was in error. And since he said it in a positive sort of way, I assumed that it meant something was pleasant."

"Yes, 'cool' means that something can be cold, but it can also mean that you like something, you are commenting on something and judging it to be brilliant."

"Oh, well then. Cool!"

He laughed once more.

"Did I use the word correctly?"

"Yes, don't worry, you totally did."

"Brilliant."

He opened his car door for me. I got in, almost falling in the process. He got in the seat next to me with the wheel in front of it. As I began to look a little queasy, he noted my expression.

"Does it smell bad? Sorry, sometimes I eat in here."

"No, it's just, this is my first time in this sort of thing."

"Oh yeah, you were unconscious in the ambulance and you only rode the bus thing before that."

"Indeed, and now that I have had time to adjust, I quite like that bus compartment. It was cool."

"You know, if you want some other words, some synonyms for the word cool, there is other terms like 'awesome', 'wicked', 'fantastic', 'bloody brilliant', and 'spectacular'."

I repeated the words to make sure that I got them stuck in my head.

"Brilliant." I remarked, "Is there anything else?"

"I am certain that there are some more terms, but they don't come to mind right now."

"What if I don't like something, what do I say?"

"Well, I don't know all the American terms, but one universal one is 'crap'. If you don't like something, you can say it's crap. And another term, mostly used in Britain, but Americans understand it well is 'rubbish'. If you don't like something, you can call it rubbish."

"Rubbish and crap."

"I shall tell you a few more terms for the day, and tomorrow, I think I should be wise and help you master the trade of using sarcasm to your advantage."

"Oh! Tell me a little bit now. Yet of course I know what sarcasm means, it means the use of words that mean the opposite of what you really want to say especially in order to insult someone, to show irritation, or to be funny. Therefore, I do know what it means mostly."

"Good, so when I say in a bored tone, 'great! I've never been so excited'."

"It means that you are truly bored out of your mind."

"Good. Sorry, I suppose I should have known that sarcasm was popular in the 1800s, since back then, words were your highest form of entertainment."

"Yes, they were. We had other sources of amusement sometimes though besides reading of course."

"Theatre?"

"Yes, and sea-bathing."

"Did you ever sea-bathe?"

"No, I never had the pleasure. Yet we loved to travel places. In fact, my Uncle and Aunt Gardiner had been saving up to take me to the Lake District back home."

"Oh, so you have never been there?"

"No," I replied, wistful, "I had not."

"What's wrong?"

"Sorry, I just—well, what can I say but that I thought of my family for a moment, and I cannot help but think on them now."

"Sorry, I didn't mean to bring it up."

"No, it's fine," I rushed out, "it's fine." Yet my somber air was not what suited me at the moment, and I wished not to cause sadness between us, so I referred to his travels. "But you sound as if you have seen the Lake District."

"I have, and well, when I get married, that is the first place that Caroline and I will go on our honeymoon."

"How long have you both been engaged?"

"For one year now."

"What!"

☙❧

"Yes, one year. Oh, in your time, it would be quite strange, wouldn't it?"

I turned and look at his profile as he manipulated the wheel. He had a fine, patrician nose and a strong chin. "Yes, how did you both survive such a lengthy engagement? To not be able to enjoy the fruits of wedded life so soon after you both professed your love for each other."

"Because marriage is not the only way that two people can be connected. Caroline and I have been dating for four years before we got engaged, then we got engaged, and there really seemed like no rush, since we already lived together."

"You lived together?" I gasped. "Truly."

"It's the times. It very much is the times."

I pressed my hand to my chest. "Yes, forgive me. I have been watching it on the television so many times, I should not be shocked. You all have such a looser way of handling yourselves."

"That is the way it is with life, and different time periods," he said, stopping at a red light. "Either you grow into a wider sense of the world, or a narrower mindset."

"And humanity grew into a wider one," I mused, still rather stunned by it all.

"Yes, it did."

❈

We arrived at a lovely hotel and disembarked. I was still in the only frock that I had from when I had entered this new world, and I got some stares; they must've thought that I looked quite ridiculous.

"Oh!" remarked one woman who passed us. "You must be one of those historic reenactors who are always walking around. What person from history are you?"

Fitz bit his lip at this, not knowing what to say, and I, not in the mood, but still growing quickly accustomed to this statement, thought it best to play along.

"Mrs. Wollstonecraft," I replied. "She was a feminist in the 19th century who spoke out against the foolish conduct books of the time, stating them to be insipid things that stunted the female mind as opposed to enhancing it."

"Oh," the woman replied, but she clearly had no idea what I meant when I spoke of it. Therefore I smiled to her, and, as I removed my bonnet, I followed Fitz inside.

"Something tells me that it's the bonnet that gives me away the most."

"Yes," he replied, "it is. And I do not believe that that lady knew what you meant when you were referring to conduct books."

"I know. Did you know what I meant?"

"Yes."

I looked at him directly.

"Oh, all right. No, I actually don't know what they meant."

"Conduct books are very popular in my time. They are books that instruct women on how to frame their personalities so that they can be perfect wives."

"Seriously?"

"Yes."

"Oh dear god, that is rubbish."

"Indeed, absolute poppycock. And Mrs. Wollstonecraft argues that such books, aimed at only basing the female mindset on how to catch a husband, not only stunt the female growth, but also it does the reverse, giving the female mind no sense or information that can benefit her, and thus making her worse for being a wife, and not better."

"And you chose her as the character you were reenacting?" He laughed.

"It seemed like the only logical step." We entered the hotel, and when I saw the nearest waste bin, I dropped my bonnet in it. I knew that I would not need it anymore. This made Fitz laugh.

⚜

As we entered, I marveled at the look of the hotel, for it was quite lovely and expansive, and then we entered Fitz's hotel room. Once we did so, I realized that we were quite alone.

I was to live with a man in his hotel room!

When I stood there, marveling at the place, I looked quite horrified and I did not know what to do. It would have been rude and improper to ask him to spend money on me further by asking for my own room, but it was necessary. And then the idea struck me quite well, and I was fortunate to have thought of it.

"But Fitz?" I asked, "We are to share a room. And yet your wife would not adhere to this. I mean, your fiancée. This would be incongruous of me to not be sensitive to her feelings."

"You're right, and that is why I have already paid for your room next door."

"Oh, thank you." Relieved, I gave him a warm smile. "And I am aware that I owe you a great debt by doing all this for me. Please, I must be allowed to tell you once more, that I know you are taking a large risk by assisting me, and also taking a great leap of faith in believing me. Therefore, understand that I do not forget it or take it for granted in any way."

"I know, and it is not inconvenient for me," he answered, not smiling, but his eyes looked gentle, so I could only assume that he was sincere. "Really, it is not. Besides, you are helping me, somewhat."

"Am I?"

Fitz's eyes darted back and forth, and he grew a little fidgety in manner.

"Don't worry," he replied. "I merely like the idea of life turning upside down at the time. After all, if you exist, then that means…"

"That time travel is possible."

"Yes, exactly. And that is a strange idea," he said, getting a faraway look in his eye, "and a wonderful idea."

"You look at me as a discovery?" I inquired, a little wary.

"Well, yes, but a good one."

"Very well. I am happy that you also get something out of this then, and it makes me feel less in your debt."

"Yes." He shrugged and clapped his hands together. "Perhaps it is time that I showed you your room, and also how to work certain… appliances."

"Appliances? Oh, you need not worry, for I was trained on how to use a—toilet, when in the hospital. And a sink."

"Yes, but have you learned how to use a shower?"

"Oh, I have heard of a shower bath before, but no, I never used it. They usually put me in a bath tub, because of my injuries."

"Good, now come on then, and there shall be a small kitchen in your room like it is with mine, so I'll show you how to use the stove and everything."

"Awesome," I commented, and he smiled approvingly once more.

⊙⅍ঠ

When he showed me the shower, I do not deny that I was a little amazed. He instructed me on how to work the knobs, and then he showed me what light switches worked where and how, what channels on the television meant what station—which was bloody brilliant, for I was soon quite addicted to certain shows, among them being shows like 'Supernatural', 'The Goldbergs', and 'Blackish'."

"Indeed, darkies have come a long way," I said, "to have their own show."

"Darkies?"

"Oh, what's the term for it? Right, negroes."

Fitz bit his lip.

"Right, I comprehend those are the words of your time, but in this era, do not call them that, for that's very offensive. Call them ethnic, African American, or African wherever country they are from, or a person of color."

"Oh, well that's…a lot of terms to remember."

"I know, but those are the politically correct terms. So you like that show?"

"I love it!"

"Well, when I was growing up, there was one show that I absolutely adored, and it doesn't come on anymore. It was called 'Living Single', and you would've loved that. I had a mad crush on one of the characters in it."

"Crush?"

"Oh, it means that I was, well, I was quite smitten with her. The character's name was Max. Short for Maxine. Don't worry, she was a female."

"Well, of course I would have deduced that, after all, what else could she have been? A man?" I laughed, which was immediately followed by Fitz's frown. "What?"

"Right," he said. "Well, that is a lesson meant for another day. Now, I'll leave you alone for some time, so you can get settled. Will two hours be enough? I know that you might want to take a shower and get acquainted with the space yourself, but then I figured that you would like to join me in my room, and we can have some dinner brought up."

"Oh, I would adore that!"

"Excellent."

With one last look, Fitz left me alone.

Taking a shower for the first time was quite a shock. Literally when the water fell on me, I recoiled and knocked into the wall and bruised my arm. Yet once I grew accustomed to it, using the small bar of soap and one of the wash rags, I quickly grew to love it!

Indeed, if we had such a thing at our disposal in Hertfordshire in 1812, then I would partake in a shower almost every day. We had heard of shower baths in our time, but none of us owned one, so it was quite the commodity.

I also let the water fall onto my hair and unfortunately had no way of drying it, but when Mr. Darcy came to invite me to dinner, and I apologized for my appearance, he said that it was not rude at all, and therefore all was well.

At last, we sat down in his room and food was brought to us by a servant of some kind, up from the kitchens. When I thanked the man, he smiled at me kindly and then left.

"You don't have to thank the hired help."

"Why did you not thank him for his service?" I asked innocently.

"Because he was merely doing his job, he's paid, and when we leave here, I shall leave him a generous tip, so why should I thank him?"

I raised my eyebrows as I admitted to being a little affronted by his haughty tone.

"Because you still ought to," I replied, unafraid to admit this, and he looked boldly at me. "To speak plainly, sir, the hired help are still people. You do look down on them so, do you?"

"Well..."

"Forgive me, I do not mean to offend, but when someone serves you, to thank them, well, it quite... makes their day."

"Ah, you learned another phrase of our times."

"Yes." I chuckled, happy that he was not upset with me, for I really did not wish to argue. "I overheard another nurse say that to a patient who was staying in the room next to mine."

"You're like a sponge, aren't you?"

"I beg your pardon?"

"A sponge. That metaphor means that you know how to soak up things into yourself. You are good at absorbing things."

"Thank you, sir."

"Also," he replied, "I, well, I have been thinking, you cannot walk around in the same dress every day. Do not get me wrong, it's a nice dress, but I doubt that you really want to walk about in it, always being asked questions, and then beginning to look ragged."

"You are right, but I lack any means to pay for such things."

"Do not worry, I can help you out. Tomorrow, we can go to Chestnut Street. There are many good shops there where the prices are not bad."

"But I shall feel as if I owe you again."

"Come on," he groaned, "we can't have you walk about with that every day, now can we?"

"No, I suppose you are correct. Yet, I do not think that I shall ever grow accustomed to those things."

"What things?"

I pointed to his legs.

"Pants. They look very restrictive."

"Yeah, I can understand that, but I'll still try and get you to try a pair. Sometimes pants can be helpful, like when you're walking far, or long, or it's cold out. Pants are good at keeping you warm."

"Very well, I shall think about it, but I can make no guarantees. And," here I smiled, "how do you know how to help shop for women?"

"Oh, my mum," he said with a smile, "she loved shopping, so she took me on all her shopping outings. I got used to it."

"Did you love your mother a great deal?" I asked simply, and he looked on me, his eyes softening.

"Yes, I did," he answered simply. "I very much did. She was— well, she was quite brilliant, and she loved me a lot. More than my dad, anyway."

"Really?"

"Yes, she loved it when I went everywhere with her, and I wasn't the best at making friends when I was a child, so I liked having the excuse of always having to be near her." As we ate, he chuckled, recalling times that were long ago for him. "She loved to paint, and all that, and listen to music a lot while she did it. So, when I was little, I always sat nearby, while she listened to The Beatles and Rolling Stones songs on the radio, and I would work on these elaborate puzzles while she did it. I tried to draw like her, but I was no good at it."

"Yes," I added. "I was not very good at making friends when I was a child either."

"You weren't?"

"No, not at all. I liked to learn things, and I had a love for adventure, but I was quite the testy little brat when I was a child. I could hold grudges and be a little mean-spirited. It wasn't until I was older, in my mid-teens, that I began to learn how to improve myself properly. When it comes to being perfect, my eldest sister, Jane, was the one who was always celebrated."

"I know the feeling," he agreed, his eyes twinkling. "A cousin of mine, Richard, was the better child amongst us two. The better man as well."

"Oh, do not speak nonsense," I replied. "For if you were a bad man in any sort of way, you would not be helping me as you are. Clearly you are a good man."

"Yes," he agreed, "but not like him."

"Just as I'm not like Jane."

We both leaned back in our chairs, our mouths full of food, and we marked each other. I suppose we merely were enjoying the comfort that comes when you share a similar experience with the person who you are with.

"Did it ever hurt?" he whispered.

"Did what hurt?" I wiped my mouth with the linen napkin that had been placed beside my plate.

"When you realized that you would never be as good as your sister, for it seems like you at least had that thought once."

I placed the napkin on the table. "I had that thought often in the past. In fact, when we heard the news that Mr. Bingley had come into Hertfordshire, my family immediately thought that Jane would be the one to suit his preferences. And, now, if time is moving then as it is now, I bet she very much is making him do so."

He studied me with quite a serious face. "Did that ever hurt? Her being so special?"

"Sometimes it did, but that is much in the past. If I ever feel a slight insecurity on the matter every now and again, that voice of envy died very soon and gave way to pleasantness. Jane is perfect, she always has been, and she always will be, and I cannot be so. Never shall I be. Yet that does not diminish my self-worth, I believe. And I suppose, that when it all comes down to it, well, I would never desire to be anything else but myself. And really, would you wish to be anyone else but who you are?"

"I both do and do not. You haven't met my cousin, Richard Fitzwilliam, and if you did, you could see what I am jealous of."

"And you haven't seen my sister, Jane, but when you do, you shall admit that she is an angel, is terribly pretty, and I look so small and meager compared to her—but I love her so very much, so I understand the preference. But no, I never wish to be her, and only myself. Unto myself, I am enough. And I am glad of it now. It is only this sticky situation that I abhor. Jane is perhaps at Longbourn now, and I am here, making your life topsy turvy, and I feel ever so upset about that. But Fitz?"

"Yes?"

"Even if your cousin has much in his favor and has numerous

charms, whatever you possess may very well be of stronger substance. I wish to believe so."

"Thank you." He smiled warmly at me, and I felt a slight glow within, for I had made him ever so happy. At least I could say that I did that for the evening.

❦

"But what of your fiancée?" I asked him. "Was she like us, and had a taciturn nature to overcome?"

"Oh, Caroline was always popular, judging by the reports of her family," he replied, his smile dropping somewhat. "Yes, I suppose that she quite makes up for my shortcomings. She always is the one talking at parties and I do not have to contribute much to anything. In fact, I bet that she prefers it that way."

"Oh well, as long as you both fit, in whatever way you do, then that is delightful. And after all this time, clearly your opposite natures are for the best. Oh, and have you mentioned me to her yet?"

His eyes lowered.

"Fitz?"

"Right, sorry. I just keep forgetting."

"You keep forgetting?" I kept my voice light.

"Yes."

"Right." I didn't believe him. "Well, whenever you wish to, I hope that she will forgive me for being such a dreadful imposition."

"She—will."

"Indeed," I replied, not convinced by his tone. "Well then…"

We both continued to eat and soon we both changed the subject to other matters of graver importance—like what television shows I would like and how I would be able to use the thing on it called 'Netflix'.

# Chapter Eleven

## MISS BINGLEY

The next day, Fitz indeed did take me clothes shopping and I desperately needed assistance half the time by the dressing room women, because I often didn't know how to put any of the clothes on properly. Yet I had fun nonetheless, and he was incredibly patient all the while.

As we walked around, and I shopped, I demanded that he ought to buy something for himself, so that the day did not focus around me, and he gave in and bought a nice shirt from a men's store. He also insisted that I purchase a couple of fancy dresses, in case I needed to attend some event of any kind. I did not see the logic of this, but since he was willing, I gave in, and then began to have a merry time with it, for the dresses were quite delightful.

One nice dress that I tried on was so glorious, that when I showed it to Fitz, he faltered for a moment, muttered that I looked quite lovely and then blushed.

"Like it much, do you?" I laughed merrily, feeling lighter than I had felt in days, and then we went and purchased it. By the end of the day, I had purchased enough clothing, shoes and undergarments to last me roughly ten days. Not only that, I chose a couple of evening dresses.

I walked out of the shop wearing one new outfit and I placed my dress in the bag after I switched clothes. Fitz had a quaint term for it.

"Well done, Elizabeth, for you have gone quite native."

☙❧

That evening, we once more had dinner in Fitz's bedroom, for we had eaten lunch out at a restaurant called 'Marathon Grill', and so we just wished to remain indoors afterwards.

"This is the one thing that is so much in comparison to my own times," I remarked, "for when we dine at hotels and inns, you can go to the dining hall, but you mostly choose to eat in your room."

"Oh, so this whole room service thing is an old custom?"

"Yes, dating back for generations."

In the middle of dinner, I had to remove myself and use the washroom. While I did so, I heard a voice from without, and it did not belong to Fitz.

"Mr. Darcy," came a mechanical voice, "you are receiving a call from Miss Bingley now."

"Oh, thank you, Gillian," he replied, his voice shaky a bit, and I froze, for I sensed that it would be the worst time for me to intrude, so I waited. Where the voice came from, I knew not, but I knew I would find out eventually, so I remained quiet and merely listened as Fitz began to speak.

"Caroline," he said. "How are you?"

"Well enough, but the florist is a complete numpty, Fitz!" The apparatus made her voice come in as clear as if she were in the room with us. "And she totally made a right hash of the arrangement."

"I'm certain that it shall be fine, dear. Do you want me to look at the designs at all?"

"No thanks, for you and I both know that you really don't want to."

"Come on, I really do."

"Nonsense. I know when you are lying and it's not your thing."

"Are you sure? I know I can stay butting out, but maybe you would be less stressed if we both did this together and I may not be the best at this sort of stuff, but I can give it a merry go."

"Fitz, you know very well, that you are no good at this sort of stuff."

"True, I'm a right side worse at it than others, I suppose."

"Oh, and I have something else that I have to talk with you about. I didn't mean to do this without telling you first, but I was in quite a bind at the time and I knew that you wouldn't care."

"What?"

"Well, my boss at the magazine needs me to fly over to New Zealand to do some cover articles on their new modeling show, and you know how much this stuff means to me."

"I know. And by that, you mean to push back the wedding."

"Oh, please, Fitz, you know that I am eager to marry you and all that. Don't forget that I was the one to do the proposing, you know."

Upon my word—she proposed to him?

⚜

What a strange thing, for I had never heard of such a circumstance occurring! Yet it was so, and Miss Caroline Bingley, who in my time I had never met, had proposed to Fitz, and he had said yes.

However, these were different times, therefore all was possible then. Yet in that moment, I had to admire Miss Bingley, for I did not believe that I would ever have had the courage to propose to any man. Indeed, proposals were not a woman's province. Yet, now they could have been. How interestingly eccentric.

And yet, while I did enjoy the idea of being able to have been liberated in that fashion, there was much of Miss Bingley's tone that I could not find so very agreeable. She appeared to be the sort who was a little too cold. Yet, perhaps that is the way it is when you are with someone for very long; you take pleasure in loving them and tormenting them. For my parents would do it on such a customary basis.

I grew misty-eyed for a moment, for it would not be in the present tense. My present circumstances implied that they had been dead for over a hundred years, which means *had done it* on a daily basis.

Refocusing my attention, I turned it back to the conversation and remained being forced to eavesdrop.

"But it is not the wedding I mean to push back, for I can't change that now. After all, I have planned everything to perfection, I believe. It is merely our honeymoon that I shall wish for us to hold off on."

"Oh." He sighed. "But I was hoping to have gone immediately afterward. I am dying to see Spain after the Great Lakes."

"But Fitz, you've already gone there before. So what's waiting a few months?"

"But that's just it. Whenever we say a few months, things get delayed, then they get pushed back further and further, and then next thing I know, we'll be going on our honeymoon after three years."

"Fitz, please…"

"What?"

"Don't be so stubborn."

"I thought that you liked how stubborn I was."

"I said that back before we dated," she said, laughing. "Yet now that we are engaged, I have quite changed my mind."

"Have you?" Fitz sighed.

"Yes, I believe I have." She laughed and it was not a pleasant sound. "And I do not like it at all." Then her tone turned somber. "But please, Fitzwilliam, for me. You know that I shall make good on our honeymoon eventually in a few months. This is my job, it's important to me, and to us when you think about it. If I get this job done well, then I shall gain more influence at the magazine and then I'll get that promotion, and then I shall also get my own spread, and more money for us."

"You know that I have enough for us."

"You do, and it's brilliant, but you can't really be serious, can you?"

"What do you mean?"

"What I mean is that, well, are you implying that I am not to put my career first at all? Are you saying that I shouldn't take it seriously?"

"Of course I'm not saying that. We're equals in this, definitely, but we planned this together. Why do this to me now?"

I listened to this conversation intently; it amazed me.

"Fitz, please don't make this personal. I'm not doing this to you. I'm doing it for you. With this spread, I can get our clients to always use your company as their advertisement agency."

There was a momentary silence at that.

Fitz said at last, "Right, that would be good, but...well, I suppose if you think it shall help. Yes, you are right."

"I knew that you would see it that way, and that's why we fit so well."

"Yes, yes we do."

⊛⋞⊛

By the time they finished that discussion, there was to be a wedding without a honeymoon, all was smoothed over and Fitz turned the situation to other matters—mostly the problem of me.

"Caroline, dear," he began, "I have something to tell you, and this explains why I have been here in America for so long."

"You're not meeting with companies?"

"Oh, I have been doing my share of that as well, but a few weeks back, there was an incident."

"What sort of incident?"

"Well, I was in a car accident."

"Fitz, why didn't you tell me? I can see that you are fine, but truly, how does the car look?"

"It looks fine, Caroline."

I raised my eyebrows. Why was she so occupied with the state of the car?

"Still, Caroline, the woman, her name is Elizabeth Bennet, and when the accident occurred, she was attempting to save a child. Yet there were side effects."

"And what was that?"

"Her brain is impaired. And her memories are disjointed. She has forgotten much of her life, even who she fully is. She knows her name and where she comes from, but that's it. In recompense for hurting her,

I thought it best to look after her. She is living in the hotel and I'm paying for her room."

"Fitz, you cannot be serious!" Miss Bingley screeched. "You didn't?"

"Caroline, what was I supposed to do?"

"Oh, I don't know; don't be such an easy target."

"What?"

"Fitz, how do you know that this isn't some sort of a trick or scam?"

"It's not, I can tell. The woman is really quite lost, and wishes to only be home. I'm looking after her until she becomes stable and I cannot just throw her out on the street with nowhere to go."

"Fitz, she's not your problem."

"Yes, she is in part."

"But Fitz, she'll eventually become so attached to you that she shall always want to freeload off of you, and mark my words, that will have a sort of change for you. She'll turn into a leech."

From my hidden spot, I seethed at her comments.

"But Caroline, tell me, where would she go? If I don't look after her, then she won't know what to do."

"All the better for her, for she'll have to make her own way. Besides, she could have just stayed at the hospital of course and they would have seen she ended up in the correct facilities."

"She is confused and lost, but not insane, Caroline."

"I just—this is supposed to be our time, and I am sorry. I'm just protective of nothing getting in the way."

"She won't. I just wish to look after her until she has gotten back onto her feet. This won't impede anything."

"Oh, you are probably right."

"Yes, I am. But this shall be brief. She is only staying so that I can look after her until she has a place to go."

"She doesn't have any family?"

"When she was found, there was no identification found on her, and she doesn't really know where she comes from."

"She really suffered from all that memory loss? Wow, this sounds like it came right out of a film script! It almost is too much like it."

"Caroline, I can assure you that she is telling the truth."

"Accepting that she is, you have to take into consideration that she may never get better. And what then? You'll have her thinking that she has a right to depend on you."

"I'll cross that bridge when I get to it. What I really wish to do now is to have you meet her. She is nice."

"She's here now?"

"Yes, but not in the room, for we were eating dinner. I swear, that's all that we were doing."

"Fitz, really!"

"I promise. I just wanted you to know why I have to help her."

"But why you?"

"Well, because it is me."

࿗

Eventually Caroline finally agreed to meet me, and Fitz came to the bathroom door.

"Elizabeth?"

"Coming," I replied, then I put on a brave face, opened the door and confronted him. As I did so, he whispered to me.

"You are about to meet my fiancée. Do me the favor and don't tell her that you believe you travelled through time and woke up in a different century. Just tell her that you suffer from memory loss, and that you hope to be good soon."

"Right," I whispered, "of course."

I approached the place where he was, and it turned out that she was speaking to him on his device—which he whispered was his laptop, and then I came face to face with his fiancée for the first time, Miss Caroline Bingley.

"Good evening, Miss Bingley," I began, smiling gently. "Hello, I am Miss Elizabeth Bennet."

The awkwardness of the meeting was clearly felt, for I had met her through a device that I didn't even understand. She was quite handsome in feature, but this was eclipsed by her look of superiority, and immediate distrust toward me. She smiled in return, but it was forced. It was clear, to the trained eye, that she found discomfort at the sight of me, to which I was not surprised. From all that I had overheard, she was quite the—complicated character, to put it mildly.

"It is nice to meet you, Miss Bennet," she said, and then she squinted. "Wait, have we met before?"

"Indeed, we very much could not have. I believe that I would have remembered you."

"Yes, well—but, something about your face feels familiar. Yes, I do believe that I have seen you before."

"My love," Fitz confirmed, "there could be no way for that to have occurred."

"Well then," Miss Bingley answered with a sigh, "perhaps you are right, and I merely am thinking of someone else."

"That is a perfectly natural mistake," I allowed. "And forgive me for being such a terrible imposition, but your fiancé has been the epitome of kindness and accommodation. Truly, you ought to be ever so proud of him."

"I am," she answered simply.

"Yes, well," I continued, not unnerved by her stiff demeanor, "might I also congratulate you on your most joyful news. You clearly shall be a happy woman."

"I very much shall be. I am quite possessive of Fitzwilliam, you see, and so I am eagerly looking forward to our wedding day."

"As you should."

"Do you have a significant other yourself, Miss Bennet?"

"Indeed, I do not."

She laughed, a light airy sound. "Well, if we meet, I really ought to do something about that. Here in London, I know a barrage of the best society in the place, and you'll be forced to meet new people."

"Thank you, I shall look forward to that when *we* do eventually come."

"What do you mean?" She asked, her pleasant tone dropping immediately and giving way to subdued alarm.

I looked to Fitz, who noted the sudden change, and then he stepped in.

"Oh, my dear, as you can tell, Elizabeth is from England, and while she cannot recall her history, I was hoping to bring her back there to stay with us, in hopes that it shall jog some of her memory. She at least recalls that she was from Hertfordshire."

"Indeed," I encouraged. "Fitz was simply kind enough to invite me to return, on hopes that I shall remember who I am. And if I am so fortunate, then I shall be able to be removed from his society and he shall be relieved of me as a burden."

Miss Bingley smiled at this, but she was silent for a brief second, and there was an awkwardness.

If I knew such awkwardness, I knew it now. She wished to squash me as if I was an ant under her boot heel.

# Chapter Twelve

## A PROMISE

Yet her look did not last for long, for after I excused myself from them both, informing her that I was retiring to my room, I left the gaze of Miss Caroline Bingley behind, knowing full well that Fitz did not hear the end of it.

As I left the room and walked down the hall, I wondered at the coincidence rather than care of her reception of me. I cared little of what she thought except that her word, naturally as a fiancée, had persuasion over Fitz. I was proud of him in that moment, I am bold and shall admit, for he stood by me when she demanded that I ought to be cast off or not to be trusted. Yet how long would it last for, I knew not.

But the coincidence!

In Hertfordshire in 1812, we were given news of the arrival of Mr. Charles Bingley with some company, and now I woke up in 2016, meeting a Mr. Darcy who was engaged to a Miss Bingley, and there was no Mr. Bingley to be seen.

There was the similarity of name, but not gender or relationship. I had gone too far into this reality to think it was ever a dream, therefore there was no point in believing that my mind had concocted this—but nor was I mad or in error. I knew what was true, but didn't know how all had unfolded, and I wondered if I ought to speak with Fitz about it.

Why had I fallen out of a reality where a Mr. Bingley moved into the neighborhood and then emerged in a time where Fitz would be engaged to a lady version? What was fate trying to say in this particular instance?

For clearly, it was trying to say something.

That evening, as I prepared for bedtime, my mind kept wandering over to Caroline Bingley, despite itself.

I tried not to think of her when I was brushing my hair.

I tried not to think of her when I pulled on my nightgown.

I also tried not to think of her when I looked at myself in the mirror by way of a moment of self-reflection.

And I certainly tried not to think of her when I clipped my toenails with a toenail clipper—indeed what an ingenious invention.

And I very much tried not to think of her when I was laying down in my bed, hoping to fall asleep, but to no avail, for I could not help but ponder the woman I had just met.

Sadly, I knew that something had to be done, and that was that something about her nature intrigued me. Painting the portrait of a person's personality always was a favorite pastime of mine, and with a character such as Caroline Bingley, she did linger in the mind.

Yet she lingered in the way that she was the sort of woman who showed how unfair life is when love and romance are in the mix—and how stupid men and women can be in the midst of it.

Fitz was a great fool to ever have proposed to her! Oh—to have accepted her proposal, I mean.

She was a gossipy socialite if I ever saw one in the course of my entire life. While I met her in the process of an intimate conversation between she and her fiancé, and naturally they would have the comfort and ease of not always having to say something pleasant or charming, for marriage sometimes seems to be the moment that charming circumstances end in certain couple's lives, should she not have been

—happier? Warmer? And attentive to his wishes for a sooner honeymoon?

I was learning the change of the role of the working woman in society, therefore I was doing my best to expand my comprehension, but her plans seemed to border on the extreme. Also, even after she had discovered the true situation between Fitz and me, she still held coldness within her, and she did not want him to assist me. That bordered on heartlessness—monstrous coldness, and I did so wonder at how she and Fitz met. It would not be indelicate to ask him, that was for certain, but there was one thing that struck true in the matter:

She was not good enough for him.

As soon as I had the thought, I was resolved to remain wary of Miss Bingley, especially since she was insistent that she had seen me before. There was no way of that being, but her wariness to believe me, her willingness to have Fitz cast me off, her worst sentences uttered that he ought not to care for what happened to me made me quite irate. Had the woman no heart?

Thus, I lay down on my bed and attempted to sleep, yet I could not initially. For every time that I closed my eyes, I saw the cold eyes of Miss Bingley as she stared at me through the screen, and a strange foreboding came over me. I felt, in some way, that that woman would do everything in her power to destroy me eventually. I had no evidence behind this belief, but I felt that I didn't need any. I always believed in first impressions, and thus I was confident in my assertions and convictions. There was something dubious about her nature... and of the coincidence. If I were to wake up in this time period, why was it Miss Caroline Bingley that I had met?

The next day I came from out of the shower to find a letter under my door, that clearly was slid underneath. Knowing that it could only be sent from Fitz, I smiled happily and lifted it up. When I opened it, any anxiety subsided when I read its contents.

Morning Elizabeth,

So I was thinking, that ~~sense~~ since we shall shortly leave for London in a five days, (sorry, but yeah, that's when we are leaving—Caroline expressly wished for me to be in London soon, but I have to be getting back to work anyway) how about I take you down to Historic Philadelphia so that you can see the historic sights? It would be a waste to not show it to you. Besides, it might make you feel better to see all that stuff, because it might have you feel closer to your times. ~~Regeny~~ Regency times, I mean. I think you will like it. There is lots of free programming there, and also there are some tours that I think you will enjoy. A lot of it is centered around the Revolutionary War and that same rubbish, where they rebelled against Britain and were really happy about it—but really, it's not offensive, because Americans often actually adore us and think we're bloody brilliant and all that. Literally, you can be the ugliest person ever, but if you have a pretty good English accent, they automatically find us interesting and cool.

I really think you'll like it. Pick up for breakfast.

Sorry, I meant I'll pick you up for breakfast in about twenty minutes. That's enough time for you to get ~~redy~~ ready, right?

Fitz Darcy

When I finished reading it, I chuckled.

"Oh, Fitzwilliam Darcy! You cannot write a letter to save your life!"

In twenty minutes, I prepared myself and was ready when I heard the knock at the door.

"Well," Fitz said as he helped me into a taxi cab, "there is no real reason to ever drive in Historic Philadelphia—literally it would be a stupid idea. So once we get there we can walk everywhere. Unless it shall make you tired, then of course we can return back to the hotel anytime."

"Oh no!" I smiled. "I am very fond of walking."

"I suspected as much." His eyes turned warm.

"Did you?" I laughed. "And why, I wonder? Am I that easy to understand?"

"Yeah, I could tell your nature after a while of knowing you."

"You presume to know me well at this point?"

"Well, I did hit you with my car."

"Yes." Although it certainly wasn't a funny event, I laughed. "Yes, you did. Oh dear, why am I laughing at that?"

"Because tragic things can be comedic in hindsight."

"Yes, once the sting of the experience has been quite done away. And when all the smoke from the disaster has been cleared, and there are only stories to be told. Yes, stories can heal a lot, can't they?"

"I suppose it is, because stories are humanity at its most innocent form."

"And what do you mean?"

"Well, Miss Bennet, it's different in your era, but in our times, things are so technological, and we care too much about the screens we have in our pockets or at home."

"Sorry, I do not understand what you are referring to."

"Oh, forgive me, I mean our phones, televisions and computers. Things become very impersonal in that way, and we humans are so cut off from each other. Technology is like a balm for us, and because we always wish to go to it, it holds us from being bored in one moment, keeps us from being idle, yes, but it leads to us not always being able to understand…"

"What?"

"How to communicate," he replied simply. "We often have no idea how to talk to each other. And therefore, when things become so impersonal, and we become closed off, when you ever do things on the internet, people can be so mean, or don't express themselves properly. What I mean is, we are in a digital age, where people don't really know how to truly talk to each other. We have no idea how to communicate."

When he finished, I gurgled lightly, and he noted it.

"What?"

"Oh, Fitz, if you only knew…"

"What do you mean?"

"I suppose maybe the digital age does enhance these flaws in humanity, but sir, you need not blame your age of history so completely. In truth, people ALWAYS have terrible issues when it comes to communication. In our times, it is so rare to say what you really feel. All must be pleasant, and what is unpleasant to talk of is not suitable for us women to speak of. Yet it must be spoken of. I mention the horrors of the slave trade in one room, and every woman does not wish to speak of it. I mention how we still don't have the right to vote, and again, I scandalize everyone. By the by, do women have the right to vote now?"

"Yes, you have for over a century now."

"Oh brilliant! I shall remember that! Yet I come from an age where it is hard to say what one feels, unless what one feels is ideal to speak of. Yet we people are not ideal. Sometimes one wants to scream and shout, and you are in an age where that is allowed. And sometimes, we are still not allowed to communicate all that is in us. All because it is not proper. I suppose, while you blame technology, I blame society.

"The fact is that something shall always get in the way of us all communicating properly, and that is ourselves. We'll always find some restriction. I suppose, because your age makes things impersonal, it is easy for you to miscommunicate and be mean about things, but in our times, because one must always be pleasant, it is easier to not communicate at all."

"Our situations therefore are the same, despite being so different?"

"Aye, despite being so different. Feel better now?" I asked.

"I suppose that I do."

"Besides," I added with a smile, "I have been in this time for no more than a couple of months and I absolutely adore the television and shaving utensils. I cannot fear the evils of such brilliant things!"

We laughed at this, and as we did, I noticed how his eyes quite lit up when he guffawed. He did not laugh very often, therefore when he did, it was quite a pleasant sight. And then his eyes fell on me and we both looked at each other fondly. I could not comprehend what he was feeling, yet for my part, it was comfort and ease. I marveled at how far we had come, how he had grown to accept the impossible when I landed in his life, and how he defended me against his fiancée. I suppose, that I hadn't appreciated him as much until that moment.

"Fitz, thank you again."

"For what."

"For being different, I suppose."

He smiled and looked down.

"Sorry, but I suppose—I should tell you, for the longest time, I was absolute rubbish when it came to talking. I was not good at all at communicating."

"Did you try to improve yourself?"

"Yes."

"Well then, that is the hardest thing in the world. You're braver than I, Fitz."

"Am I?"

"Yes, yes I suppose that you are."

۞

We entered Historic Philadelphia, got a free map from the main tourist center, then Fitz looked on the map, circled places that he thought I would have an interest in seeing, and drew them in straight lines so that we could have direct routes to where we would go.

As we walked around the historic sights, from Christ Church (A place that I had known much about, for of course, Christ Church had initially had its roots in England for quite some time) to Carpenter's Hall, we went, and I enjoyed all.

Christ Church was my favorite because the tours that were given there were quite lovely. There also was the Betsy Ross House, which was the home of the woman who made the first American Flag, and there were historic reenactors there as well to represent people in history. It really was quite enjoyable.

Then Fitz expressed merriment when we came upon a bench where there was a storyteller who was offering to tell free historic stories.

There, we heard about a woman named Alice, who was a 116-year-old woman in 1802 who people would come and see to write down her stories as a context for what happened in Colonial America. There was another storyteller at another bench who told us about how George Washington—during the war—lost many battles, but he found a dog that belonged to a British general, and he was kind enough to return it to the general. Then there was the story about how a woman named Sarah Hale had continued to write to the presidents to make Thanksgiving a holiday for over a decade before they said yes. With that story, I enjoyed it a lot, but I had to ask Fitz what Thanksgiving actually was.

"I'm not entirely sure," he answered honestly, as we walked away from that other storytelling bench. "That's an American Holiday only, and we don't celebrate it in Britain. When we get back to the hotel, we can look it up on google."

"Google?"

"Oh, it's a search engine you can look up stuff with on the computer. Which reminds me that I should really start teaching you how to use one."

"Thank you; that would be great."

"One thing that we learned though is that Thanksgiving definitely has a turkey involved."

"Yes, it sounds…barbaric." I squelched a shudder.

"Oh, but I do believe that they really just eat it."

"Oh, well that, that is another matter. Delightful."

Afterwards we went to more historic sights, and went to a few more storytelling benches to hear stories there, including a story about two sisters named Sarah and Angelina Grimke who fought for the abolition, the story of Benjamin Franklin and the first Fire Department in America, another story about the laundry process of the 1700s, and how it took three days to do it, and then we ended our story at Independence Hall, where we heard the story of a woman named Harriet Tubman.

When we were there, I looked on the building, and surprisingly, being there held much significance for me.

"There." I pointed. "On the other side of this building, that's where we first met."

"Yes, it is," he whispered, following my gaze. "Two English people, from two different time periods, who met in the place that America declared its independence from England. For anyone who loves irony, this is quite colossal."

"I cannot account for it, but I am happy," I confessed, smiling sadly.

"Yes," he responded gently, "like I said, ah, the irony."

To eat dinner, we went to Market Street and dined el fresco at one of the restaurants near the river. Afterwards, Fitz took me to an ice cream shop called The Franklin Fountain and when he saw my shock at there being so many flavors, and my relief that there was no tomato flavored ice cream, he was quite amused.

"There really was tomato flavored ice cream?" he asked.

"Yes," I responded, "and oyster flavored ice cream as well."

"Sayeth what?" He gasped, playing on classical Elizabethan era phrasing.

"Indeed, perfectly normal." I laughed at his expression.

I then ordered the maple walnut flavored, Fitz ordered the coffee flavor, and we left the establishment with our cups of ice cream, with me marveling at the taste of it along the way.

"Astonishing!" I cried as I ate a spoonful. "After eating this, I shall never be able to have the ice cream of my time, for it does not taste this good."

"Well," he replied, taking a spoonful of his coffee ice cream, "if you ever do return."

When he spoke this, I felt halted. My insides had felt as cold as the ice cream. I had not thought on my absence from home for some time because it hurt to think of it, but never did I tell myself that I would never fully return. I suppose, I chose not to think on it. When I was silent for some time, he noticed, and it ate away at him.

"Forgive me," he rushed out. "Did I hurt you?"

"It's fine," I answered hurriedly—too hurriedly.

"I see."

We walked on a little further.

"Miss Bennet, Elizabeth… was that last reply of yours a reply that you did not fully mean?"

"Indeed, it was not sincere," I confessed. I looked at him and then I smiled. "I see. With you I must be entirely open. Your last acknowledgement gave me pain, not because you offended me, but because, I suppose, that I have been running from reality. I suppose, that if I chose not to think on it, I could deny the possibility that I would never find a way to get home again. I had a blind hope that I followed really well, and it gave me strength, but time has quite ate away at that concept."

Unable to hide what I felt, my voice began to lower as I grew emotional. "And now it comes time to speak, and I find that I do not know what to say. I suppose, that I am quite sad."

"We don't have to talk about this here. Hold on."

He went to the curb and waved down a taxi that was coming down the street, we went into it, and then we drove back to the hotel. Along the way, we were silent, for I didn't know how to form my thoughts, but Fitz seemed to understand that I just needed a little bit of quiet at that time.

Eventually we arrived back at the hotel, we entered, and he invited me into his room so we could have some tea. To my surprise, when we entered, he did not order it, but rather, he pulled a pot from a cupboard in the kitchen and began to boil some water.

"You're making me tea?" I remarked.

"Yes, for water is something that even I cannot destroy with my bad cooking skills."

I laughed gently at his quip and then he offered me choices from a cabinet. I chose the flavor 'lemon lift', and he prepared it for me.

"Thank you," I offered. "For I do not really think that I was fit for being in public at that precise moment."

"I know the feeling."

"It is quite vexing, isn't it? To be that person who cannot hide one's feelings."

"Yes," he concurred. "Emotions can be like a time bomb. And they can always go off in the wrong place."

"Yes, they can. But we are alone now, and I should not be afraid of talking about what I really feel, should I?"

"No, you shouldn't," he agreed.

"Thank you. Well, I suppose, that it is beginning to occur to me that I may never go home. Could you imagine that? Not ever being allowed to go home? And also not being allowed in the time that home was?

"My parents, mama and papa, and my sisters, Mary, Kitty, Lydia— and Jane. Longbourn, and my Aunt and Uncle, the Gardiners. My Aunt Phillips, and my friend Charlotte Lucas—all the experiences that I have had in my life, and they are quite gone from me. And not just at a distance, no but out of time, out of place, and world. I am separated from it all, and they are all ghosts now. They are all just moments of moments past. I'm a memory to them. And they are a memory to me."

"I cannot imagine how you feel."

"No, you cannot. But what you can do is clearly be brilliant at making tea."

Fitz smiled, placed my teabag in a mug and offered me some sugar.

"Oh thank goodness you have real sugar and not that sweetener stuff!" I took a spoon and poured myself some. "It was offered to me once at the hospital and I cannot imagine how you all eat it, for it is quite rubbish."

"I agree."

"Of course you do."

"And what does that mean?"

"Well, you don't strike me as the man who would like things that are not…real. In any way."

He bit his lip and took that moment to sip the tea.

"Oh, I do like this flavor," I said, "it is delightful."

"Yes, yes, it is."

Eventually, it came time for me to head to bed, so I cleaned my mug and as I prepared to leave, Fitz opened the door for me.

"Elizabeth?"

"Yes?"

"I should ask."

"Yes?"

Fitz looked down at his feet and then he chewed his lip.

"There's something you have not thought about."

"And what is that?"

"You mentioned the possibility that you might never get back home. That you will be stuck here, having to assimilate, get a job, a flat in London maybe and learn how to live. I know that's hard, but you clearly have it in you to survive such a change. And yet, what happens if you do actually return home? But what if you do find a way to get back?"

"Well… I would be happy of course."

"Well, naturally you would be able to see your family again, but after being exposed to all this. After learning so much about the future, your present, well, it would feel like the past for you. Do you think there is the possibility that you can never fully go back?"

At this suggestion, I could not shut away the implications to his assertion.

"You're referring to the fact that I have too much foreknowledge," I summed up. "You think, because I have had a taste of this era, I cannot fully return to my own."

"It's possible."

I gazed down the empty hallway. "You're right, it is. I shall know so much. I shall know that we will lose this next war with America. I know that I shall perhaps not live to see women be allowed to vote. And no one would listen to me. Yes, I do see what you mean. There would be so much here that I shall miss. But there is one thing I think that shall give me solace."

"What would that be?"

"I will have my family back; they are not supposed to be my past. My family is meant to be my present. And I shall be able to return and see them anew. I will be able to be a better older sister to Mary and

Kitty, and I might even be able to grow more affectionate toward Lydia. I will see Jane find her happy ending, for I believe that she will. And I suppose, I shall care more, for the future keeps one from taking things for granted really. And there is something else."

"What?"

"If I go back, I can find that one thing that is closest to your heart."

"What?"

"Fitzwilliam Darcy."

"What?" he repeated.

"No, I mean, I can find out about the missing Mr. Darcy of Pemberly in 1812. I can find out what happened to him. And for your sake, sir, I'll promise to look after him."

# Chapter Thirteen

## LOOK IT UP ON GOOGLE

After I said this, he shrugged, not knowing how to take it.

"What's wrong?" I asked.

"Well, it is just…if this is all real, which I have no choice but to accept, then if you do find him, and then you look after him, time will change."

"Yes," I whispered, amazed at this concept. "Oh dear, well that is a little intimidating."

"Yes, it is, and most disconcerting and interesting. It does frighten me a bit, that my entire history can change. Will I remember the change, or will time just be completely unwritten, then rewritten?"

"Oh, this discussion has led down a dark path," I replied lightly. "To unwind knowledge and then fall directly into the unknown. And what if I cannot remember any of this? What if when I fall back in time, I can't remember you. Oh, dear god, never mind, let's not—it doesn't matter."

"No, I suppose that it doesn't."

"But if that be so, if time unwinds everything, then I'm sorry that we cannot help each other through it."

"Me too," he answered. He pressed my hand gently and then I returned to my room.

Once more I could not fall asleep, so I turned on the television, went to the movie selection and re-watched a movie I had seen four times already, 'Thor, the Dark World'. Not understanding why it was not considered a very good film, I lay in bed with the lights out, hoping to fall asleep over time, and just as one character held another, repeatedly saying the words 'I'm sorry', sleep finally found me.

The next day Fitz began to teach me even more of how to use a computer and by the end of the day, I had mastered how to use Google, Yahoo, and YouTube. The next day, he offered to show me how to open a Word program and then how to use it to write certain things.

"If you can't work a computer," he said, "then you cannot survive this world. I'm not perfect, but well, even I understand the concept of teaching a man how to fish as opposed to just giving him one."

That evening, he had ordered us tickets to a tour called Independence After Hours, where we would dine at a place called City Tavern, then we would be given a performance, then walked to Independence Hall by a person playing a historic character, and then we would be given another performance there by other reenactors.

When dining at the tavern, Fitz actually let me convince him to choose the turkey pot pie for a meal, which he had never had before. We both enjoyed it immensely and the tour was quite fun.

The second to last day there, he took me shopping once more so that I could have a couple of coats for if the weather in London ever began to take a turn for the worse, which it could always do without the slightest provocation.

I suppose that I surprisingly recall my time in Philadelphia with perfect clarity and detail because—it was the calm before the storm came.

Troubled waters lead to interesting tales and gripping yarns.

But calm waters are what we always remember with fondness.

The next day brought the day of our departure and we had our bags packed, took a taxi to the airport that was outside of the city and that was the first time that I had actually seen an airplane. I had heard them overhead many times, but this was my first view of one.

"Fitz," I gasped with trepidation when I saw one fly off the ground when we were in a gate terminal, "we really are going to go into one of those?"

"Yes, we are," he replied, most amused. "Don't worry. They have these bag things on there in case you ever feel sick."

"But—that thing could crash?"

"Statistically, planes are the safest way of travel actually. Oh bollix! Now I sound like Superman!"

"What?"

"Never mind. Don't worry, I promise it will be fine and remember, I'll be sitting right next to you every step of the way. Well, it's more like every meter flown all of the way rather than step, but you know what I mean."

"Yes, I do." I breathed in heavily, trying to prepare myself. "Indeed, right now, I really do just miss that boat that I woke up to on the river."

"Sure you do." He sounded amused.

Eventually it was time to board the plane, it was a long and tedious process which really was quite aggravating. In truth, with all the preparation that went into traveling, I wondered that anyone did it, because it really took a lot of energy. Once we were on the plane, I felt very confined—despite that there was more space on the plane than in a carriage. I sat in my seat, looked at all the passengers and then all was assembled.

And nothing happened.

And more of nothing happened.

"Why are we not moving?" I whispered.

"Don't worry."

"Is something wrong with this strange machine?"

"No, this is normal. Oh, and I forgot to tell you this, but when we take off, if you have the impulse, try to resist it."

"Resist what?" I was cautious.

"Try your best not to scream."

"Oh. Right. Well, I think I can do that."

Eventually there was a sound as stewardesses came past us and checked to make sure our seat belts were secure, then the pilot talked to us through a radio—or at least I thought that was what it was, then we finally began to move onto an air strip. At present, I had found it actually quite fun, so I felt that there was no need for alarm, until the airplane began to pick up speed, and as we lifted off the ground, I quite forgot myself—and I did scream.

Yet luckily, he was quick to act, and he apologized to me as he placed his hand over my mouth.

Now we were going to London, England. Back to the place that was home for both of us.

# Chapter Fourteen

SOMETIMES, WHEN YOU'RE A WOMAN, THE
SCARIEST THING CAN BE…ANOTHER WOMAN

And to England we had arrived. Once I had gotten used to the feeling of compression in the airplane, I adjusted to the plane ride quickly, to my surprise, and then hours upon hours later, we had crossed the ocean and since I had the window seat, I was able to look out and see Britain from below.

"You took to the plane ride very well after a while," Fitz said as he helped me retrieve my carry-on bag. "You didn't throw up once."

"You sound proud of me." I chuckled.

"Well, it is a small kind of accomplishment, I suppose."

"I take my accomplishments where I can find them, and my compliments, so thank you."

We disembarked, had to retrieve our bags from the baggage claim and walked along the airport.

"I should have mentioned," he interjected, "that we shall be picked up."

"Oh, by who? An employee of yours?"

"No, by Caroline."

"Miss Bingley?" I suddenly felt quite frozen inside.

"Yes. In time, you shall call her Caroline, I believe."

"I'll wait for the invitation to do so," I replied evenly, "but hopefully she shall let me do so in time."

"She will, don't worry. Caroline is like a cat—slow to trust but she grows warm in the end."

"Whenever we fed a cat well enough, trust was easy to gain," I offered. "And I have no delicious stories or connections to feed her with. I just—what if she doesn't like me, Mr. Darcy?"

"Don't worry, she's not going to cook you and eat you. Everything is gonna work out."

I smiled diplomatically, but I had my suspicions. Whatever way Miss Bingley and I would be introduced, it would not be as anyone would desire, I felt.

⚜

We reached another hall after the baggage claim and there were many people waiting. In the multitude, there was Miss Caroline Bingley, holding a bouquet of flowers and one rose. When Fitz accosted her, I held back slightly and allowed them their moment to be alone.

"Fitzwilliam!" Miss Bingley cried. "It has truly been too long my dear! I missed you every waking moment."

"I missed you too," he replied, then he took her in his arms, and I had to look away as they kissed passionately. I thought my unease with witnessing their moment of affection was intrusive and perhaps impolite of me, and therefore I continued to look to the ground, not wishing to look back until they had done. For some reason, my stomach felt suddenly empty and I felt a moment of sickness. I grabbed my midsection, clutching my stomach and rubbing it to settle whatever momentary queasiness that seemed to develop.

"Elizabeth." Fitz's voice came from my side. "Are you all right?"

In hearing him, they must have ceased their public displays of affection, for he was now talking. I turned to him, seeing Caroline out of the corner of my eye behind him, and he did look concerned. Seeing his expression, I immediately softened.

"It is the strangest thing," I elaborated. "I felt sick all of a sudden, an unease in my stomach, and I cannot account for it."

"Ah, perhaps it's the after-effects of air-sickness." He turned to Caroline Bingley and took her hand, just in time for me to turn and note her expression. It was one of wrath, quiet resentment and bitterness. It was quickly erased by one of pleasantness when Fitz turned back to her, but it was too late for me. I saw her look, and it would not ever be forgotten. "This was Miss Bennet's first plane ride, Caroline, and she did well."

Caroline looked on me with a forced smile.

"I did my best, indeed," I said. "But he helped calm my nerves when we lifted off the ground for the first time. I was so shocked that I felt as if my stomach might fall into my knees."

"I can well believe it, for that is what my first plane ride was like," she added, "when I was six years old."

"Oh, you flew that early."

"I'm surprised that you did not ever fly at your age, but then you are English. So how did you ever go to Philadelphia if not by way of plane?"

I flexed my hand, nervous, for I had no answer. As I thought of how best to lie in this situation, Fitz came to my rescue.

"A very unique way," he fibbed. "She actually took a boat ride, a cruise from the UK."

"Yes," I agreed quickly. "I may not recall much of my past, but luckily when I was found, I had a boat ticket on me to indicate this."

"Ah, saved by paperwork." Caroline smiled. "Those are the times, aren't they?"

"Yes, I suppose that they are."

"Oh, and I have this for you," she said, and then she handed me the rose, "to welcome you back to England and also for condolences for your accident."

Despite my knowledge of her true nature, I was still moved by the gesture and therefore I took the rose with eagerness.

"Oh, thank you, Miss Bingley. Truly, this is very lovely." I put it to my nose and smelled it; again, there wasn't much scent, but I appreciated the gesture.

There was a moment of awkwardness between us, for indeed I had no idea of what to say, and neither did she. Fitz, therefore, urged us onward and we began to head toward the exit, to Miss Bingley's car.

"So," Miss Bingley began, "I am quite curious. Miss Bennet?"

"Oh, if you like, please, you may call me Elizabeth," I offered, hoping this would bring some ease between us.

"Oh, cheers. Then you may call me Caroline of course. And I hope that we shall be good friends throughout your stay here."

"Thank you, Caroline, I believe that we shall."

I knew that there was no way that we would ever be friends, because if there is one thing that quite kills any genuine camaraderie, it's beginning an acquaintance saying that we shall be good friends. After that, everything quite becomes forced.

"So, as I said, I am quite curious, how much do you remember of your previous life?"

"Well," I said, picking my words carefully, "I do remember being from Hertfordshire, I remember walking around Meryton, the town right near it. I remember a house. A lovely house, and I recall faces, who I suppose were my family. Fitz has been very kind and has suggested to take me into Hertfordshire, where hopefully something will awaken some memory of some sort."

"It was also recommended by the doctor who oversaw her at Jefferson Hospital," Fitz added. "Anything, including time, would be able to awaken some memory of hers, and then we can take it from there."

"Well, your accent," Miss Bingley said, "it's very proper. You must have had a very illustrious education."

"Actually, I can assure you, that it is very much not so." I laughed with ease. "In fact, my mother was not a slave to our education."

"Your mother? So you do remember her."

"I remember a face," I answered smoothly.

"But what do you mean in that she was not a slave to your education? Were you home schooled?"

Fitz explained. "Elizabeth, what that means is that you were taught at home and did not attend a school for your education."

"Well, yes," Caroline said, looking at me in a confused way. "You didn't understand what I had meant?"

"My apologies." I felt myself blush. "Forgive me; some things are still very unclear. The little that I remember is that my sisters and I did not attend school. We were merely taught somewhat at home."

"Oh, you were home schooled, that can account for some things."

"I beg your pardon?"

"You seem to have a very sheltered way about you. A very simplistic nature that is quite charming."

"Oh, thank you," I said, even though I knew that half of what she said was really an insult that she covered up. I looked to Fitz as well and he flinched—I think he also knew.

"But perhaps I am being very annoying right now," Caroline continued, "for here I am, questioning you, when you must be very tired from your trip and you are already in a perplexed state. Really, I wish to know you better."

"Oh, that is perfectly understandable, and I can assure you that I am not tired at all. Besides, it is very good to ask questions when you first meet someone. It only means that you are curious about them."

"Precisely."

"And it is always good to be curious," I added.

"Yes," she laughed, "yes, it is."

"Besides, this gives me the chance to inquire as well. Tell me, for I am quite curious to know. How did you and Fitz meet?"

"Oh, this is a story that we have been telling people over and over for years," he said.

"Yes, and as you can imagine, Elizabeth," Caroline interjected, "that while Fitzwilliam has grown weary of talking about it, I still love to tell it for it is my favorite story."

"And that is perfectly normal," I encouraged. "Telling a love story is a woman's trade, therefore we must keep it in practice."

"True. True."

৩৯৩

As we journeyed home, Caroline then began to regale me of their love story and how they met.

I suppose that I had been quite spoiled by novels, because I guess that I had expected something more unique about their tale, but there wasn't.

They had met at a dinner party that was being held by Fitz's aunt, Mrs. De Bourgh, and then they met a couple more times in town when the magazine that Caroline worked at needed to use his marketing company to help advertise them.

After a couple of meetings, Fitz asked her on a date, she said yes, and then they kept dating. Eventually she proposed and the rest was history.

Indeed, it was as simple as that. And yet, I suppose that it always ought to be as simple as that, for anything else would be unreal.

As we drove through London, I did not speak because I was mostly preoccupied by staring out of the window. Fitz told me I could roll down the window if I liked, and he showed me how to do it, to the critical eye of Caroline, who noted that I needed assistance to do it, but I cared not. When finally able to roll down the window, I heard the sound of a very different sort of London that I was accustomed to. The noises were so different, and the sight of it!

Everywhere there was life, cars, buses, the buildings were endless! I saw the clock of Big Ben in the distance. We drove past many clothing stores such as H&M, 'Dolce and Gabbana' and a slew of others, we rode along the Thames, St. James Park, and everywhere there were more people than there ever had been in London.

And to think, I had thought London was overpopulated in my time, but this was—it was as if London was the center of the world.

As I stared out at the city, we pulled up next to a bus that had two stories. Being so used to Septa's bus design in America, this was very different than what I had been accustomed to.

"This bus here," I said over my shoulder. "It's got two levels."

Fitz chuckled. "Oh, yes. In London, we have double decker buses. You'll like them."

"Yeah, they do look positively smashing." I laughed, completely forgetting myself. "I would love to ride one. But really, this is London! I would never have dreamed this! Look at it. It's like this is the whole world in this one city."

"Still wonder why I prefer the city over the country now?" He chuckled.

"Oh shut up, Fitz!" I laughed. "Besides, in the country, you can still take long walks."

"Elizabeth, you can do it in the city still. As a matter of fact, you are perfectly right to walk as far as you want in London, for as long as you like."

"Really?"

"Yes, it's proper. And it's endless of what you can see here. Compared to it, Philadelphia is small—well, smaller anyway."

"My god." I still sighed, overwhelmed at the sight of the place. "Look at it. I cannot take it in so simply. Yes, I wish to walk as far as I can. I want to see everything. Oh, forgive me, I sound greedy. And—"

I turned around and saw Caroline looking at me, her eyes like slits as she stopped at a red light.

"You've never seen London before?"

"Oh, well, um, no I have not. Or at the very least, I do not remember having seen it so."

"Very unique. In the whole course of my life, I do not ever think that I have met a person here in England who has never once come to London. Your parents must've been true homebodies."

I thought quickly. "My mother—well, from what I recall of her, my mother would not have minded coming, but my father despised town."

"Town?"

"I mean London."

"Oh, you are also the first person to refer to London as a town."

"Oh, is it not usually called that?"

"No, for it's too large." Caroline Bingley laughed. "It's a city that's a world unto itself."

"I can well believe it," I replied, looking out of the window once more and taking London in. "What is that tall building there?"

"It's called the Shard," Fitz replied.

"It is immense! And I love it."

Fitz chuckled, and Caroline managed to emit a brief smile and laugh.

"Your freshness to this all is most amusing," she allowed, "and quite refreshing."

"Well, I hope to provide good company. Especially since I am being such a terrible imposition."

"Oh, not at all, Elizabeth," she replied, in a way that I could very much not believe her.

She then turned to Fitz and they began to talk of her magazine business and his work, while she also spoke of the wedding. At first I was attentive, listening in to learn what I could of Caroline's magazine business, but very quickly I grew a little bored with it, so I turned and continued to look out of the window.

Whatever was Caroline's profession, I could learn more of it later, but for now, London was the most intriguing subject to learn about.

※

Eventually we arrived at their townhouse which was in the area of London called Mayfair, and the neighborhood was the epitome of the word 'smart'.

"This area of London was named after the annual May Fair which used to take place here, am I correct?" I asked.

"Yes, it was," he answered as we pulled down on the street where they lived. As we had ridden along, I took in the appearance of the very luxurious hotels, restaurant and shops.

"Well, this is all very…"

"Posh?"

"Oh, well, that word is new to me."

"Oh, it means rich and fancy looking."

"Yes, well, that's the word for it. Posh. Posh—that word sits so strangely in the mouth. Yes, but with you all, I should not have expected you both to have lived anywhere else, but the best."

"Actually it was our third choice," Caroline said. "At first, my dear Fitz and I could not agree. I wanted to live in Marylebone."

"And I wanted to live in Notting Hill," he commented. "This was our compromise."

"Oh, well it is very lovely all the same."

"It's closest to the best area of London," Caroline said. "And therefore I can always settle for second best." She gave Fitz a look. "But I always look for the best in the end."

I looked away, afraid of any intimate reaction that they could be having at the time, and then we pulled up in front of their house. When we did arrive, the house looked very 'posh' and perfect. Large and beautiful—everything to symbolize their income, but I couldn't tell…it just didn't feel homey from without, but it would feel so from within, I supposed.

I complimented them on how lovely it looked, and Caroline was satisfied with all my praise as we entered the home. It was lovely, very clean, and everything looked as if it was in its proper place. Indeed, I was afraid to sit down, for fear of making anything look out of place there.

◈

At some point, while I was shown into the guest room, I was unpacking my things, and all the while, I had a sense of dread. I feared the inevitable of eventually having to be in Caroline's company while Fitz was not present. I quickly got the sense that he brought out the kinder sides of herself, and sadly, I was proven to be correct even before I expected so, because before I finished putting my clothes away in the dresser and closet, there was a knock on the door.

"Come in," I said, hoping it was Fitz, but knowing who it really was. The door opened and Caroline appeared. Caroline was lovely, to be sure. She had beautiful chestnut brown hair, gray eyes, and a lovely figure. In truth, she was quite handsome.

"Hello, Elizabeth, I just came to make sure that you are settling in well enough."

"Oh, I am, thank you."

"You're welcome. And I also must tell you that dinner is at six pm. You will find our cook to be quite the talented chef."

At first, I thought to be polite, but I knew that it would only make the distance between us even larger, so I thought it best to immediately attack the heart of the matter.

"In truth, Caroline," I murmured with a sigh as I sat down gently on the bed, "at this state that I am in, I could be given a cheesesteak and find myself to be the most fortunate creature in the world. Forgive me, that was something I ate in Philadelphia a couple of times. They actually were bloody brilliant, but I knew it might not have been the healthiest of things."

I laughed nervously, looking away from her. "In truth, when I came back to England, I was hoping for things to immediately be put to rights, and I would be able to find and fall back into my own life, but as you can see, that is very much not what happened."

She leaned against the door and crossed her arms over her chest. "What do you remember?"

"Bits and pieces, but nothing to help me see anything with clarity. In truth, Caroline, I am very lost, I suppose." I picked up a decorative pillow from the bed. When I turned to her, she looked at me strangely.

"What is it?"

"It's just, your face is so familiar. I could have sworn that I had seen you somewhere before."

"Forgive me, Caroline, but I do not believe that is possible."

"How would you know? You cannot remember half of what you have experienced."

"I suppose that you must be correct in that," I allowed, "and yet I feel as if I would have remembered you. But if so, and I do not recall us ever meeting even if we did, then that is more frightening."

"More frightening? How?"

"Because if I met you, and I can't remember you, then nothing might trigger my memory, and that frightens me. Yet, if you say that you have seen me before, then do you remember our encounter?"

"Oh, it's not that I think that we met, it's just your face. It seems so familiar."

"Oh, that is all?" I laughed lightly. "Well, my face is not an uncommon one, I suppose. You very well could have seen my face and it just belonged to another."

"Yes," she said, but her eyes sparkled in a way that I could tell that she was clearly not convinced. "Yes, perhaps that is it. Now there is the other matter."

I was cautious for her to continue. "And what is that?"

"What will you do if you do not find out who you are? For surely you cannot expect to live off of the generosity of my husband forever."

⛬

I noted how she called him her husband and not her fiancé, which was good of her, but for some reason that I could not account for, I didn't like it.

"No," I replied evenly. "I know I ought not to, and I have dreaded being an imposition for as long as I have been."

"Fitzwilliam feels indebted to you because of what he put you through. He feels responsible."

In truth, it was much more than that, I secretly thought, but she would never understand, for I got the sense that she was a woman with little to no imagination.

"It is a natural response to hitting someone with one's car," I magnified. "His feelings of obligation show his greater attributes then. After all, what sort of person would be so malignant that they would not offer to assist someone that they hurt who needed their help? That is hardly humane affection, now is it not?"

I groaned inwardly. Here I was, in the home of Miss Caroline Bingley, and I was not afraid to be direct and impertinent. That was so positively me in every way, but it could not be helped.

I had overheard how she advised Fitz to abandon me, and I could not ever forget it. Yet if I didn't say anything to alter her mindset, she would not see that she was in error—and yet, I still was in her home. Therefore, I could not tell if my statement was correct or too presumptuous. Either way, Caroline Bingley had never learned that I had overheard her, so my statement was merely one that sounded like naïve innocence, luckily.

When I finished my declaration, Caroline looked down at her hands, and then she bit her lip. Therefore, the only thing to do was find the wisdom of changing the subject.

"Yet back to what you suggested, I do not mean to trespass on the hospitality of your home for very long. I was hoping to find a way to gain employment in some way."

"What are your skills?"

"My skills?"

"Yes."

Now it was my turn to be thoroughly confused. All of the usual accomplishments that a lady ought to possess in 1812, (well, the little bit that I did master), now seemed so pointless. Who cared if I could play the pianoforte a bit? Who cared that I could sing a bit? Or sew somewhat? I could read and write, naturally, but not enough to make me a governess of any kind. After all, the world had greatly changed since my time. Whatever knowledge I possessed had been obsolete for two centuries. My goodness, the definition of an accomplished woman in 1812 now seemed to be quite...useless.

Even if I had learned to paint, I still would have not much to make me special. How trivial it all felt now, what was considered important back then? Now, in that moment, I did comprehend what Fitz meant. After learning all that I did, how can I go back to the world that once was?

🐌🐌

Yet, still to the point and purpose, I had not much to recommend myself in that moment, therefore I searched my mind to find what I could offer, and there was one thing and one thing only. After all, I had often looked after Kitty and Lydia with Jane, and I also would oversee my cousins, the Gardiners, when my aunt and uncle would invite me to Gracechurch Street. And that concept, that occupation, was surely an immortal profession. After all, the world may change, but children would always remain as children in any era.

"I do have some skill at being a nanny," I said, "from making sure a house is maintained and the children are supervised."

"Oh, a nanny. Yes, those are always in high demand. Then again, there are many young women who can do it, and it is an overstuffed pool of applicants for it."

I didn't fully understand half of what she said, but I assumed that she meant that there were many women who applied for half of that position.

"Well," I began, "I suppose that I can find a way to put a post somewhere, such as in the newspaper."

"Oh, barely anyone who is socially in sync with the times reads newspapers. It is all online articles these days, and also agencies. Yes, there are babysitting and nanny agencies that we can get you registered in so that we can find a post for you as soon as possible."

"Thank you, Caroline, that would be lovely."

"Very good. Yes, and that way, if you do not have a home, at least you can stay with the family. As nannies do. And if you have no other skills, at least you do not need many to do that."

I took her meaning quite well and bore the insult as best as I may.

"Well, if I prove to be up to the task, looking after children does require a skill, just a different sort."

"Yes, I suppose so. Well, I shall leave you now and will see you at dinner."

"Thank you, Miss Bingley."

"Miss Bingley?"

"Oh, forgive me. Caroline."

She nodded to me and left.

And that was my moment where I was finally able to exhale, releasing all the anxiety that I felt around her.

❧

Eventually it was time for dinner, so I went down and met them both at the table. At first it began comfortably, but then Caroline turned to subjects that were between her and Fitz and had nothing to do with me, so I was able to mostly observe them.

At first it was well, for they spoke of the wedding and I was content in hearing the plans. Then Caroline began to talk of preparations for her magazine, where I expressed a desire to see one of her copies, for I would like to know what went into publishing one.

And then it grew to be quite uncomfortable in some ways because Caroline began to touch Fitz on his face, and blow kisses at him, which was of course proper in the 21$^{st}$ century, and I was quickly growing accustomed to it. Yet whenever they did so, I grew apprehensive, a little repulsed and needed to continue to look down at my food, becoming quite engrossed with the pattern on my plate.

Yet, above all, I suppose the seed of my discomfort sprang from Caroline, whom I knew in my heart that I could not trust. Sometimes when you're a woman, the scariest thing can be another woman, and I feared her for some reason.

Little did I know at the moment…just how right I would turn out to be.

# Chapter Fifteen

## LOTS OF NOTHING, LOTS OF EVERYTHING

The next day, I woke up to a knock on my door. It was Fitz, telling me that the cook made some breakfast. I slipped into a dressing gown, because I didn't want to keep him waiting, then I went down the steps to eat, and found him sitting there alone. To my satisfaction, Caroline had to leave early and go to a studio to overlook a model that was posing for a magazine. From what Fitz gathered, Caroline disagreed with the outfit that the model was going to wear initially.

Therefore, with ease, I sat down next to him and began to eat voraciously.

"Hungry?" He laughed.

"Well, now that I do not have to worry about manners in any way, I am not afraid to show my true appetite. In truth, Fitz, I love to eat."

"And I love hearing that. In our times, all we ever hear about is how a woman is worried about how many calories that she has consumed throughout the day."

"Counting calories? That is counting what nutrients and what not is in food, correct?"

"Yes."

I paused with a forkful of eggs half way to my mouth. "I find that I could not do that. I do not have the self-discipline."

"And that is well and good."

"Thank you, so I forgot to ask. What church shall you get married in?"

"Oh, St. Paul's."

"And afterwards, will you at least spend time in Pemberly before she has to get back to work?"

"Perhaps not."

"Really? Tell me truly, Fitz, do you never really ever wish to go there?"

"What is your fascination with Pemberly?" he inquired curiously.

"Do you want the truth?"

He sat back and studied me. "Sure, why not?"

"Well, it is the only thing that I learned about the other Mr. Darcy," I confessed. His expression altered, as he was clearly affected by what I spoke of. "You see, I never met him, and I know that angers you, because I cannot tell you what happened to him, but where he comes from is all that I know. And besides, our times were so very different. A man's identity was quite attached closely to the maintenance and size of his estate."

Fitz leaned back in his chair, blinking.

"Far be it from me to groan at the importance of wealth, for I like being so well off," he proclaimed. "But is that right, Elizabeth? Why should a man's identity be so wrapped up in his house? Don't you see the shallowness of that?"

"You and I come from different times."

"Time should not determine such deviation of thought and theory though."

"I see your mind and mindset, Fitz, but that is the thing. The size of a man's estate places value on his pocketbook, which can always be a little mercenary. I confess it to be so and even that it may not be just or right, but it is more than that."

"What else is it?"

"Well, it is not just enough for him to have a great house, but it is also how he runs it. And how he cares for it. The Mr. Darcy of 1812 seemed to boast of Pemberly and cared about it. It seemed to just be… him. All of him. Therefore, that was the only impression he gave. And if he overlooked his estate, cared for it, cultivated it and made it prosperous, then he would show a steadiness of character, a consideration for things, responsibility, and a care for his lineage. He would care to live up to his father's name and accomplishments."

"Ah, the whole living up to our father's name and accomplishments." Fitz sneered. "Yes, that is always quite cumbersome."

"I suppose that it can be. Yet that is what it means to consider a man's estate as much as you care for the man. His home can often be an extension of his character."

"And show that he is just filthy stinking rich," he interjected.

"Something that you are," I returned the jab. "For god sakes, Fitz, have you woken up grumpy today?"

"Oh, am I being grumpy?"

"Yes, you are. What's wrong?"

"I don't even know. We men, when we wake up in bad moods, we don't even know half the time why we are having them."

"Oh, that excuse!" I scoffed. "Fitz, that is such a false reason, because it's an easy one to use. Really, you must be more original."

"Oh, very well, I guess I should stop being grumpy. Today, I believe that we should stay home, so you can relax now that we are back, but I could imagine that you would want to see the sights."

I brightened immediately. "Oh, I very much would love it! This is London, but it's not the London that I am used to."

"I need to find a day to take you, but I was wondering about something Caroline spoke about to you. She told me that you would be interested in gaining employment as a nanny."

"It seems like the only thing that I might possibly be good at. Because I really have no other skills that shall help me survive in this time."

He nodded, stroking his strong chin. "She spoke in a way that hinted that she would like to find a post for you immediately. Elizabeth, forgive me, but I get the sense that you do not want to get a job so very quickly."

I lowered my gaze. "You're right, I don't."

"Of course you don't. You had time to adjust to Philadelphia, and now you need time to adjust to London."

"But despite my best wishes, I can see that Caroline is correct. I don't want to trespass on your hospitality for much longer."

"You know that I am not annoyed by you. I'll talk to Caroline and urge her to understand that you need more time."

"But it will make her unhappy. To speak plainly, Fitz, Caroline doesn't like me."

He appeared about to disagree, when I added, "Oh, come now, you know it."

Fitz bit his lip and then slowly nodded.

"She can be really kind, great, and my fiancée is brilliant in every way, but she is merely being possessive right now."

"Of course, because she views me as a threat."

❦

When I spoke this, I did not flinch, nor was I afraid of Fitz's reaction, for we had reached the moment where we were used to being so frank with each other.

"And what do you mean by that?"

I took a long sip of tea before answering. "Well, it is natural. I appear in your fiancée's life, claim to not remember a thing, depend on you. Also, you're rich and prestigious, and therefore, I could always be lying.

I stirred more sugar into my tea. "Also, this is Caroline's special time, and therefore she must look on me as an imposition. She does not trust me, and it's best that we talk about it so that I get in her way as little as possible."

"You are both very strong and determined women who speak clearly and with honesty," Fitz said. "That's what made me fall in love with her."

I looked down at that comment. While I allowed Caroline being perfectly natural in her reaction to meeting me, I still could not warm to the idea of her, or still be dubious of her being worthy of her fiancé.

"I suppose, since your natures are so clear and to the point," he continued, "I can see where a problem could arise. And you are right, she is uncomfortable with this."

"Well, I shall be here for a time, and I hope that she learns to like me, therefore, I shall only be around you both sparingly, and also I need your help to find a very good wedding present for you both. Presents always help."

"You wish to get along with her. That makes me happy."

"It does?"

"Yes, it does. But don't worry, I'll talk to Caroline for you, to give you more time. And I have not forgotten our plan to travel to Hertfordshire. Trust me, I didn't forget."

"Oh, Fitz, thank you!"

"Yes, we just have to make the time, because I must get caught up with all my work."

"Don't worry," I said with a smile, "I won't make you talk about work just now."

"Thank you, because I really didn't want to."

We smiled and then laughed together.

৩৵৩

Since it was our last day to be alone together, Fitz thought it wise to just have us sit in and watch television.

"Often it is said that you cannot learn anything from watching TV," he said as we were sitting on the sofa with chips and other couch food —Cheez-Its being my favorite, along with nachos and salsa which I found delicious as well. "But that is absolute rubbish! You have two hundred years of English history to become acquainted with and culture to also learn about. And there is one answer for that, and one answer only."

"And what is that?" I replied, cutting some fruit and vegetables for us to have along with our 'junk food', as he called it.

"It's called the BBC." He laughed, and then he turned on the television. "One thing England does really well is show you every aspect of our culture in some film or show or another. Also, knowing what's on television will help you adjust to the times. Shows, and their fanbases, help the world go round nowadays."

"Well, what are we humans if we do not love and obsess over things?"

"Spoken like an ideal country lass."

"So speaks the city boy." Our banter was so comfortable.

"And the current owner of Pemberly—who doesn't deserve it apparently."

I didn't know what he meant by that, but I thought I would do better not to inquire for the moment.

So, at first, we watched a few news stations so that I could gather a comprehension of current issues in England. Indeed, it was nice to know that crime in London was no different than the amount of it in my times. Well, some things just never changed.

Then he introduced me to Britain's most popular shows. The first was 'Downtown Abbey', which enlightened me on that particular era, and it was quite ideal for me because it really shed light on the time period. There were a few other shows we watched as well, including the 'IT Crowd', which helped me understand the computer age even further.

And then came the show that would change everything, and Fitz groaned.

"Bloody hell!" He sighed. "Why didn't I start here? For there is relevance."

"What?"

"We have a show about time travel."

"A show about time travel? And like how it happened to me!"

"Yes, we spoke of it before, well, actually, you fell through time somehow, but this is about a man who travels through time. Well, actually the character's an alien."

"Do you mean from out of town and not from London?"

He raised his eyebrows and gave me a look of pleasure. "No, I mean like he's from outer space."

"Oh." I shrugged. "Well, of course he is. But if it's connected to me, then what's the show called?"

"'Doctor Who'."

"Oh, yes, that show! Finally, we get back to that again!"

⚜

After watching two episodes of the show, I was immediately fascinated. A show all about something that had occurred to me. Indeed, it made me feel quite not alone and exploring the potentialities of something similar happening in my adventure. I expressly asked Fitz if we would continue just watching the show, and he took delight in it. It turned out to be one of his favorite shows, so he was content in seeing me fascinated by it. Once he explained the premise of the show, he jumped around and showed me different episodes from different seasons so that I would get used to all aspects of the show.

The more we watched, the more satisfied I was, for it began to offer possibilities of what had occurred to me. Perhaps I had fallen through a hole in time and fell here for some reason, later in Fitz's family timeline. What drew me there, I still knew not. After all, when I fell there, I heard the sound of a clock. Or perhaps something drew me to that particular moment in time. Some object, action, thing or person. Something! And it was more than Mr. Darcy simply touching me that once.

Before that day, I had no direction. Nowhere to find any suggestions of what could have happened to me, but now I had options. I could very well accept that any answer was possible, because anything had proven itself to be possible.

And if there was a way that I fell forward in time, there was a way to fall back.

⚜

The minutes turned into hours and before we knew it, we had been sitting on the couch till the sun was setting, and I had not felt as if a moment was wasted.

As we reached the end of an episode that I had liked a great deal, I looked at Fitz as it neared the end. He was sitting there, opposite me, no more than a couple of feet away, his feet propped up on the coffee table, utterly relaxed and lax in his manners, biting into a cucumber that he dipped in salad dressing. I looked over his entire form, and for some reason, just sitting there with him, doing nothing but watching TV, I somehow felt at peace—and as if I had never had more fun in my life.

Then the episode came to an end and he turned off the television.

"Caroline will be home soon. Be prepared to eat a dinner despite that we are already full."

"I can very well give it a try," I replied softly, my mood lazy and light. With my eyes, I smiled at him.

"What's that look for?" he asked.

"It's strange. But I suppose...I am just very happy now."

He nodded in agreement. "The joys of simplicity. And a good show."

"Yes. We sat here, and I felt that we had travelled all around the world."

"All around the universe. We travelled all around galaxies and didn't even leave the room," he added with a sweep of his arm.

"Yes, we did. What was that last episode that we watched?"

"The Bells of Saint John."

"I liked it," I answered, still feeling quite content.

"Yes, it's one of my favorites. Tomorrow I'll show you my other favorite, 'The Shakespeare Code'."

"I look forward to it, but you have to work tomorrow."

"Right. Blast it, I totally forgot."

"It's fine. I'll watch it on my own. But Fitz, do you think any of the theories in the show could be true?"

He appeared pensive as he answered, "I see what you're thinking. If this were a year ago, I would say that is rubbish. Yet now, with all this change, clearly this all could be real in some way."

"But this is fiction. So none of the theories they have for travelling through time actually work?"

"No, they don't. So, there is no solution yet for you."

I lifted my shoulders and gave him a shy smile. "But still, I have hope."

As we stood up, I suddenly felt a rush of gratitude, so I accosted Fitz and kissed his cheek.

"Thank you. I really did enjoy this day."

"You're welcome," he replied kindly. "And I suppose I can say that I, Mr. Fitzwilliam Darcy introduced Elizabeth Bennet of Longbourn, Hertfordshire, 1812, to the BBC."

We were disturbed when we heard the door open and Caroline had come home.

We spoke to her about our day, and unable to control myself, I talked on and on about what we watched, and at first Caroline listened politely, but after a while, I noticed her bored look and therefore silenced myself, then inquired about her day and how did her work do.

She turned the discussion to the model who's outfit she had to fix in the magazine cover for their next issue, so I asked if she had any pictures, and she was happy to produce them. When she did, I confess that I did enjoy the look of the picture and there was something quite intriguing about it. Caroline even offered to let me join her on another day where they were shooting models for a gown spread in the magazine, and I was willing to accept, hoping she meant it. Perhaps that would help us gather a stronger acquaintance.

Either way, the day came to an end, and I went to bed, tired and content, enjoying a day where I did lots of nothing, but somehow did lots of everything.

# Chapter Sixteen

## LONDON

I n a couple of days, I had desired to travel around London to see what it was like. Fitz didn't want me to go alone and asked if I would wait till he was more available. I thanked him, but advised against it, informing him that it would vex Caroline. Understanding this, and happy with me always being so upfront about things, he found the best thing to do was to hire a taxi service, where the driver also had experience with all the traveling/tourist sites in London. The night before, Fitz and I mapped out an itinerary for all the locations that were worth seeing.

"Yes, London has greatly changed since your time, Elizabeth." He chuckled when he wrote down another site for me to see.

When the day came, Fitz was kind about it as well—and I felt indebted even more—for he gave me two hundred pounds—and the taxi service would be paid upon returning me home.

The taxi driver was a man named Merrick. He had dark brown skin, and, his hair, I believed that they were called dreadlocks, were long, and he kept them tied back. He proved to be a brilliant conversationalist, but I suppose that is the way it is when one is a taxi driver. He also really loved London clearly, because when I told him that I had never visited London before, he got so excited that he began to tell me historic facts about everything that we passed that had any historic significance.

We travelled through the areas of London that could be seen in one day.

First, he took me to Bankside, where I saw a replica of 'The Globe Theatre' where Shakespeare would have put on his plays, and that was absolutely smashing. We also went to the Millennium Bridge where I saw the best view of London, and I also saw St. Paul's Cathedral from a distance and recalled that that was the place that Fitzwilliam and Caroline were going to get married. It was implied that now I was invited to it, and for a moment, I was a little melancholy.

While there, I would know no one, and I would sit there awkwardly and be so out of place, that I would be kind of an intrusion on the event. Yet I would grin and bear it well, for I must. However, I reflected on how they met and wondered how life often was like that. You meet someone at a desperate hour, tell yourself that it is an ideal match, and then date them for a long time despite any possibility that they were not the ideal candidate to marry. And then you rush headlong into the relationship, perfectly willing to know as little in advance of the defects of one's married partner. Charlotte Lucas would be quite proud of Fitz at the moment. Of course, she would also be scandalized by my calling him Fitz, therefore she would not be so proud of me.

Yet of course, it was different. Fitz and Caroline had been together for years, and yet how could they know each other so very well and not know each other at all? Yes, they were different, and sometimes difference doesn't mean disharmony, but something about their personalities, in my mind, just didn't work. And I couldn't help but despise Caroline, for reasons that I could not fully determine.

I suppose, within myself, I had to confront the idea that when they married, I could no longer have Fitz as a friend, and he was the first companion that I had made since I had come. From the day we met, he stuck by me, despite when he didn't desire to. Thus when my life would change once more, I would have to let him go, and find a way to establish such a connection somewhere else. The idea quite frightened me, but it was not jealousy, no I would not allow that. I suppose it was just something else.

Afterwards, I went to Bloomsbury, which is celebrated as the home of many a great writer, then we went to City which was its name title, then we went to Clerkenwell, which was where Caroline's magazine agency was located, but of course I knew it was not correct to visit.

We also visited Kennington, the cab driver Merrick and I ate at a restaurant in Little Venice, and we even got the chance to visit one more place in the nearby areas, which was Paddington. It was one of Merrick's favorite places.

"This neighborhood is actually famous because of a children's book," he informed me. "It's a book about a small coat-wearing Peruvian Bear named Paddington. If you want to read the book, it's quite good, and the movie version is pretty brilliant as well. Here, let's go to the Isambard Kingdom Station. It has a statue of the bear."

He took me there and in front of the public transit station, was a large statue of this bear.

"The story really must've become popular for this to get made."

"Yeah, it did, yeah."

"It looks…wicked."

Merrick chuckled at this.

"Amazing. I usually give tours to Americans when they come. You are the first Englishwoman I have taken on tour."

"Yes, well," I replied, smirking, "I suppose I lived in backwards times."

"No offense, but totally. You didn't visit London, fine, but for your parents to not even introduce you to Paddington, now that's just rubbish."

"Yes, so it would seem." I chuckled, for he would never learn that my parents really had no choice in the matter.

"Yup," Fitz said when I returned at last to their home and he paid the taxi by credit card, "Paddington was one of my favorite books when I was a kid."

"It was?" I smiled. "You never tell me about your childhood."

"Ah, well, there's not much to tell. In truth, I was a shy child."

I angled him a glance. "And so you loved books, didn't you?"

"Yes, I did."

"Well good, for I bought you something."

"Did you?"

"Yes," I replied, taking a wrapped parcel from my shoulder bag. "I know that you probably already have it, but when Merrick and I stopped at this amazing bookstore—it was positively shooting— Merrick told me that it was one of the most popular books ever. Besides, what do you buy a man who has everything? You can't buy him anything he has never seen, but only a better copy of it."

He took the parcel, opened it and it was an illustrated and noted version of the book 'The Hobbit'. When he saw that, he chuckled.

"Wow."

"Did you like the book?"

"Oh yeah," he said with a smile. "In fact, when I was a child, my mother used to read it to me as a bed time story."

"She sounds like a good egg, your mum."

"Oh, she was. I was quite the mama's boy. In fact, my other copy was so old that I had to throw it out years ago. So no, this is my first copy that I have had in years."

"Then I gave you the right gift?"

"Yes, you did," he replied, looking on me warmly. "Thank you, Elizabeth. I love it."

I smiled, quite giddy, because I was so amazed that I had found something to suit his fancy, and it did feel like a small sort of accomplishment in a satisfying sort of way.

When we had sat down to dinner, I had informed Caroline that I had visited near where she worked, including the other areas, and somehow, this struck up the idea within her to invite me along with her friends the next day, for she had a bridal fitting for herself and her bridesmaids.

The invitation was kindly meant, but I could not help but feel secretly apprehensive. Of course, Fitz was content with this plan, and between not wishing to let him down and also to be polite and cordial to Caroline, I agreed.

"Oh, you shall love it, Elizabeth," she said, "for I am not the sort who believes in my bridesmaids wearing hideous gowns. No, I flatter myself that I am quite generous in that way, for I would not hear tell of my bridesmaids wearing anything less than the very best gown they could choose."

"Yes, that is very generous," I allowed, but I didn't know what else to say except for, "I am sure that your maids agree and feel indebted to you."

"Yes, perhaps they do. For I am not the vain sort to feel that they have to be grotesque to make me prettier. No, no I am not."

She continued to talk more and more about our day; I listened with eagerness mingled with curiosity and had to accept that no longer would we discuss the sights of London, which is what I most expressly wished to ponder on.

# Chapter Seventeen

## THE GOWN

I woke up the next day in a panic, for this was the first time that not only would I be going out with Caroline, but I would also be in the company of her friends, who, if they were anything like her, would despise me very quickly or find my ignorance on certain matters worthy of ridicule.

I was, for the first time, going to be in a company of women in the $21^{st}$ century, and it felt as if I was out of my element, which was something I usually was not when I was mingling with my own gender. I was so apprehensive that I briefly met with Fitz before he left for work and asked him if he could suggest anything I could say that would help me get along with them, but he was as much in the dark as I was.

"What I don't know about women is a lot," he confessed, "despite being engaged to one. But, from what I can determine, wear something that makes you look nice, so that they could complement it. It's always easy to begin a relationship when there are compliments involved. You love television, don't be afraid to offer your preferences if they ever discuss theirs.

"Listen to the flow of their conversation," he continued, "and put in a remark whenever you find something that you can relate to. Be kind, but don't be afraid to offer your own input sometimes. And wear lovely but comfortable shoes, because you don't know if they want to walk somewhere afterwards."

"Anything else?" I asked, amused, and thoroughly confused about what he said that I should listen to and what half was him just guessing.

"Yes," he said with a smile, "try not to be intimidated."

"Oh, you need not worry about that. My courage rises with every attempt to intimidate me."

"I shouldn't be surprised."

With a coy smile, I answered, "No, you shouldn't be. Now have a good day at work."

Fitz nodded to me, and then was off, and I returned to the house and awaited the throng of Caroline's friends.

⚜

Luckily the day did not go as badly as I had anticipated. Caroline's friends were named Elizabeth Elliot, who went by Eliza, Mrs. Augusta Elton, and Miss Fanny Dashwood. While they did possess Caroline's posh nature and sense of self-importance, they did not offer any conversation that left me quite overpowered, and if Caroline had spoken any negative remarks about me, they were kind enough to hide it and not torture me to my face.

They asked me a few questions about myself, but they mostly stuck to conversations about Caroline's magazine, outfits that were premiered in the latest issue, and Caroline showed me a copy of it so that we could peruse it.

I quite enjoyed it a great deal, for clothing and social columns in magazines are immortal things that always can lead to easy conversation. Sometimes they mentioned a famous individual who they loved or despised, but I was not afraid to ask who they were and what their reasons were for loving them or despising them, and they enjoyed my ignorance and just filled me in on things.

We spoke of other subjects, but I was happy that our conversation mostly stayed light, for it helped our acquaintance along, and then we arrived at the bridal salon, where they all got dressed in their gowns.

I paced back and forth, waiting for them to get in the gowns, and observed everything around me.

"So," I whispered to myself, "this is what it feels like to get married. A lot of fuss and fun... would I enjoy this? I cannot tell."

Eventually, all the bridesmaids got into their gowns quickly and Augusta, Eliza and Fanny appeared in lovely green gowns that actually fit them quite well. When I saw them, I gasped and clapped my hands.

"You all look beautiful!" I exclaimed.

"Thanks, and we feel sexy!" Augusta cried, her arms outstretched as she twirled around. "Finally, an end to the bridesmaids' gowns that would make the blessed Mary weep with how ugly and codswallop they were!"

"Indeed," I acknowledged. "I come from a place where the bridesmaid gowns are always duly inferior, so it's nice to see a change."

"Well," Fanny said, sitting down next to me, "being allowed to be pretty certainly makes up for the bridesmaid curse."

"What curse?" I asked.

Eliza spoke. "Oh, you haven't heard of it? Here is that concept of always being a bridesmaid, but never a bride."

"Yes," Fanny continued, "where you see all your friends married off, but you are never yourself. And then you sit there, every wedding, and then you have to hear all your family asking you why you can't find a nice bloke."

"And then they look at you as if you are doing something quite wrong," Eliza said. "But Augusta wouldn't know anything about that."

"Well," Augusta said, "you both need to stop complaining and just enjoy your gowns. Being married has benefits and so does being single. Though, I do confess that I am lucky, for my lovely Mr. E and I adore each other."

Eliza groaned. "Oh don't make me puke."

"Well, my dear, then you shall just have to puke."

"But you, Miss Bennet." Eliza turned to me. "Are you seeing anyone?"

"No, I am not."

"Have anyone in mind?"

"No, I do not really."

"Oh, that is so not true," Fanny refuted, "we are always thinking of someone."

"Would I let you down if I were to deny it still?" I laughed. "Indeed, I am in earnest. I am not thinking of someone."

"Well, give it a little time, my dear, and you shall be before you even know it," Augusta put in. "That's the way it is, you know. Love always has a habit of sneaking up on us."

"Yeah, it's a foul git in that way." Eliza groaned, and then she looked at herself in the mirror. "Well, at least I look brilliant in this, but Miss Bennet, never fear, we bridesmaids have the right to be a bride eventually."

As they continued to talk on and on, I marveled at them. Here I was, almost two hundred years outside of my comfort zone, and yet the issues, the desires, dilemmas, and denials were still the same as they had always been. I suppose, no matter the age, no matter how Dickensian or digital, human nature is human nature, and passion and people cannot change.

All my worry about not reading the books they read, saw the films they did, have the same tastes, passions, and pursuits they possessed, or their prestigious professions, and I had no reason to worry in the end. There would always be some social and status difference. But through it all, everyone was looking for that one thing: human connection and affection. Love was an immortal thing, a grand thing for the romantic, and even those who were cynical. Therefore, it was always a matter of time before the subject would return to it, not because one had no life outside of it, but because it was a language that all understood.

Yet the struggles and sufferings were the same as well; it wasn't always easy to find a soulmate, it seemed. And the more Eliza and Fanny talked on it, the more it was clear that it was as hard in their time as it had been in mine. All had the dream of the perfect one, but time taught them that he may never come. Therefore, in that moment, while they were at the height of their complaints, I was amazed that I found myself to be the cheeriest of the lot, even though I came from a world where the pressure should have been worse.

"Oh, cast off this feeling of inadequacy," I advised to Fanny and Eliza, "And enjoy that you don't have to get married. I mean, it would be nice of course to have someone, but really, are we so lost because we are not found? I have learned something strange about my fortune."

"What?" Augusta asked.

"Despite what I would have expected," I said with a smile, surprising myself, "I kind of like being lost a bit. And while I am lost, I don't think I could handle love. Therefore," and here, I took their hands, "let us be brilliant about being lost, then, and be glad about it. There is something to be said for losing oneself, I feel. At least for a time."

Fanny was about to reply when the assistant announced that Caroline Bingley was finished and then she entered, wearing her wedding gown.

✦

With all speed, Eliza, Augusta and Fanny rushed to her and exclaimed that her gown was perfect, and the only thing that held me back was that she was not fully comfortable around me, but their exclamations were correct.

Whatever were her flaws as a person, her form and figure left nothing wanting, and she showed how ideal she was, now more than ever in a long and very well-designed white gown. I let out a gasp and complimented her on how she looked.

"Indeed," I confessed, "you appear now to be the loveliest woman in all of Britain."

"Well, a bride ought to be," Caroline answered, and then she looked at herself in the mirror.

Over and over again, her friends cheered for her and I remained sitting there, silent.

"I want my wedding gown to be just like it if I ever get married," Eliza said, quite forgetting my declaration a moment ago, when I was so close to enhancing their outlook on themselves. And then Augusta turned to me.

"Miss Bennet," she asked, "wouldn't you want your gown to look just like this one if you ever were to give into the ceremony?"

I suppressed a chuckle, for it would be scandalous of Caroline's gown to be permitted in the church in 1812, for it would be considered too elaborate and scandalous.

"While it is the most beautiful thing in the world," I agreed, "and it works for you, Caroline, I confess that I would not do the 'all white' gown any sort of justice. If I were to get married, I always thought to have my gown be pink, a light green or light blue."

"You don't want a white gown?" Fanny asked, confused.

"Well, it is not usually the standard unless one prefers it," I put in. "So why must I…"

I trailed off when I noticed that they were all looking at me strangely, and then Caroline quickly excused me.

"Ah, things must be different from where you are from," she stated, "for wedding gowns are usually always white."

"Oh," I said, realizing that it must have been a custom that came into fashion after my time, "forgive me, I suppose that my life was a little too sheltered. So, was this your first choice for a gown, or did you have other options before you settled for this one, Caroline?"

"Ah, there were many options!"

I sighed in relief as the conversation changed and focused back onto her.

☙❦❧

As Caroline had her dress packaged away and she was in the dressing room, getting her clothes back on, I went to her while her friends were looking at other gowns and asked if she needed my help at all.

She answered back in the negative, but still asked me to come into the dressing room while she got her shoes on. I entered and waited for her as she tied her heels.

"Sorry about my foolish comment earlier," I apologized, "for I should have known that gowns of course were white for weddings."

"Yes, well, you have recovered from an accident, so I suppose that it is another thing that you have forgotten."

"Yes, of course. Perhaps that is it."

"Well, now you know."

"You shall make a lovely bride, Caroline."

"Thank you," she answered, looking at herself in the mirror. "Do you know, when I first saw Fitz, I knew that he was just the sort of man that I wanted to marry. He was strong, tall, clear-eyed, and he understood my nature, and how I was perfect for him. Fitz is the sort who needs a woman who knows her own mind, and is resolute, firm and can be decisive, even when he can't be. That's why I must tell you, Elizabeth, that you cannot have him."

❧

When Caroline gave her declaration, I flinched and felt cold quite suddenly.

"I beg your pardon?" I whispered, "what?"

"He's a strange sort of man, my fiancé. When you meet him, he does not always give off the best first impression. Yet his spirit is like wine and he gets better over time. He grows on you, even before you know it. And so you have no choice but to fall in love with him. But you cannot have him, Elizabeth. Fitzwilliam Darcy is mine."

I literally gasped. "Caroline, while I can very well comprehend your apprehension toward me, you are mistaken. I view him as a friend, and the man who did not abandon me when I needed him."

She fluffed her hair. "Such feelings can turn into love."

"I do not know about that. All I know is that I wish for us to get along, Caroline, and that I do not want Fitz."

"What you want, Elizabeth, perhaps scares you to death so much, that you fail to realize yourself and your true feelings."

I looked down at the ground, feeling like a cornered beast, for I knew that nothing at this point could change her way of thinking.

"Caroline," I answered with a sigh, "what do you want me to say? For if I deny it, you shall not believe me, and if I agree with you, you shall despise me forever. Either one will feel like it's a lie or a half-truth.

"Well, do you want me to admit that I feel a connection to Fitz? Well, I do. I feel it because he hurt me in an accident and then cared for me, therefore saving my life. How could I not admire him for that? Do you want me to admit that I find him handsome? Well, of course I find him handsome, because he is. Do you want me to admit that I need his help? Well yes, I need his help."

She turned and gave me a skeptical look. "Why do you need his help?"

"Because I don't know who I am and where I am going. But he is helping me to find out what both of those things are."

"That can grow to love."

"Yes, it can. But there is no reason to be afraid of me."

"I shall keep telling myself that," she answered strongly, firmly, and we exited the conversation as confused as we had gone into it as Augusta entered, wondering why we were taking so long.

# Chapter Eighteen

## THE HAPPIEST DAY OF HIS LIFE

*A* *mazing*, I thought to myself, *Truly amazing!*
I had just finished reading the book *Anansi Boys* by a writer named Neil Gaiman, and it was totally wicked! Literally, it was one of the best books that I had ever read in my life. I didn't understand all the references in it, but that only made me wish to look them up on the internet and figure them out. At first, I considered picking up his other novel, *The Graveyard Book*, but I decided to give myself something to look forward to. After all, I had already read two of his other novels, *Neverwhere*, and *American Gods*, in less than two weeks, therefore, I needed to pace myself. As such, I took a reprieve by watching some more television.

"Elizabeth!" Fitz called for me from downstairs. "What are you doing?"

We had already eaten dinner and Caroline had to leave because she had to meet with a business partner of some sort. For a woman who was worried about me feeling for her husband, she was a little foolish about always leaving me alone with him too often. Fitz had gone out for a jog, and I thought he had done so to make her happy in not being alone with me while she was away, but it was clear, hearing him enter the house and call for me, that he did not care to wait.

"Elizabeth, where are you?"

"Where any woman from the 19<sup>th</sup> century would be if she woke up and found herself in the 21<sup>st</sup> century," I called.

"That means you're watching television again, aren't you?"

I giggled to myself, for he knew me well. "Of course, you prat."

"Let me guess, you're watching Doctor Who again."

"Of course, now stop being a prat."

"Do you want anything to drink while I am down here?"

"I'm fine, I have some tea."

"Right. Coming up."

"Good, because I just started this episode."

Fitz entered the room, wearing his sweat clothes and I smiled at him.

"How was your jog?"

"It's jogging." He sat down lazily near me on the couch and I offered him some apple slices that I cut while he looked at the television. "Oh, this is the episode '42'."

"Right. I love this episode."

"Me too."

"To be honest, I don't like how the Doctor treats his companion/friend in this season, because she deserves a lot better and I like her a lot."

"I know, she's one of my favorite characters."

"Yeah, I sort of know how she feels. I kind of know what it's like to go one's whole life and be bold, but always feel as if I am living in someone's shadow."

"I know how that feels too. That's why I like her as a character, because I can relate to her situation. How do you feel similar?"

I thought a moment. "Because of my sister, Jane, remember? She came out first, everyone loved her, she had the greatest disposition, and she was the great beauty of the family, and then I came out, and I use my wit to hide it, but I know the truth; I will never be regarded as being as good as she is, as I told you before."

"I'm sure that you are better," Fitz stated with gentle firmness, and it filled my heart.

"Thank you, Fitz, but if you saw my sister, you would favor her, just like everyone else does. And I bear her no ill will, and I admire her all the more for it."

He shook his head. "I don't have to see her. Something tells me, you are as good as she is. You're just different."

"And so are you—from whoever's shadow that you feel like you are living under. So," I said, raising my cup in a toast, "to being regarded as second best, but really, we are bloody fantastic."

"Absolutely fantastic!" Then we drank.

"So," he began as we were watching another episode called *Vincent and the Doctor*, "tell me. How did your day go with Caroline?"

At first, I only told him of my situation with mentioning the color of dress I would have for my wedding.

"Oh, that's right!" he said, tapping his head. "White was not the color for wedding gowns initially, was it?"

"No, it was not." I emitted a bitter chuckle. "And I googled this. The first time that white became a trend for wedding gowns was around 1840, long after I was pushed out of my time, when Queen Victoria wore white for her wedding. Before that, we didn't do that.

"For our weddings, we just wore our best Sunday dress, or if we had a gown made, we would choose any color that we liked. White was not often chosen. White only symbolized that you were rich, because it indicated that you could maintain it looking clean by having someone always washing it. So, when that occurred, oh bollix, I felt like quite the fool." I briefly put my face in my hands.

"I feel like I should have warned you about that somehow."

"Oh, don't be down on yourself, I forbid it at all costs. There was no way that you could have thought of that."

"I suppose not."

"Caroline told me something though."

His interest obviously peaked, he asked, "What?"

"About when you first met. She said that she knew, when she first saw you, that you were the perfect man to marry."

"Did she?" He seemed quite pleased.

"Yes. And I wonder, what were your first thoughts of her?"

He stroked his square chin as he thought of his answer. "When a man meets a woman, that is never what he thinks usually. I know, not very romantic, but so it is. When I first met her, I just didn't think anything."

"You didn't, huh?"

"Like I said, not very romantic. But so it is. When I met her, I thought she was smart, nicely dressed, and suitable, but there was no initial attraction. Time had taught me that one."

"Well, I suppose, when it comes to love, it's not how you start, but as long as you get there in the end."

"Yes, wisely said, Elizabeth. Quite right. Quite right."

He took a swig of his beer and looked at me.

"What are you thinking?" I asked him.

"Forgive me, I just want to know what else."

"Pardon?"

"How did you both get on? Are you getting along better?"

"Fitz, for a moment, I thought we were, but it was not so. She still very much doesn't trust me."

He leaned back against the sofa. "Oh, I'm sorry then. It was my hope that you would get along better."

"Oh, I wish we had not let you down then."

"Yes, well. Something tells me that you did try, and I can ask for no more than that."

"Thank you."

It made me happy that he did not blame me, as it also made me feel comfort in that he had wanted me to get along with Caroline, but some things just could not be overcome so easily.

❧

The days leading up to Fitz and Caroline's wedding rolled on. I learned how to work a computer, gained secretarial skills, and Fitz even taught me a little bit about how to drive—but he was not that successful.

Finally, the day of their wedding came. They married in St. Paul's Cathedral, where I would learn that Fitz had mostly distant relatives and friends because he had no real immediate family. Yet this was quite made up for by Caroline's family, who took up three quarters of the church of those who were invited.

The church was impressive.

The bride was elegantly dressed.

The bridesmaids were not duly inferior, but only slightly so in their gown choice.

Caroline's father stood in the pew, torn between an expression of contentedness and boredom.

Caroline's sisters could be seen looking at their flowers in their hands and fidgeting with their gowns, worried that they looked disheveled.

And Caroline's mother did not even try to cry.

That made me happy, because one does not always need to cry to show joy and I would much rather prefer it if the scene did not arise if it was not real.

Caroline, however, did try to cry when she reached the altar, but eventually her emotions just were not going to pour forth, and she let her face rest between contentment and eagerness.

With all important preparations of hers, she was complete, between a restlessness to get married, nervousness that comes with a wedding day, and breathlessness that came from a gown that hugged her so tightly that it sucked her in, and I believe made her lightheaded.

Marriage indeed can be a stressful business.

Yet on her special day, I wore the best gown that Fitz bought me and as he waited for her to appear at the end of the aisle, I rested my eyes on him. He breathed out and in nervously, and then wrung his hands. I suppose that he was worried at her standing him up, but I knew that he worried for nothing. As his eyes scanned the crowd, finally his gaze rested upon me. To lighten his mood, I made a quick face at him and he chuckled. Then I mouthed 'good luck' as well and he understood and nodded.

This day was the happiest day of his life, and I suppose, I had no choice but to be happy for him. Eventually the wedding march was struck up and Caroline marched down the aisle with her father, and how ironic it was that I was present—a woman who she warned not to look at her fiancé not three weeks before. Yet now she would catch him in full, so I suppose that she no longer looked on me as a threat in any way.

The ceremony progressed, and the sermon was not long, but it was long enough, vows were exchanged, rings as well, and then at last, came the kiss that sealed their marriage. Once more they kissed passionately, and I could not stop myself; I bit my lip and looked at my lap.

I had to force myself to join the clapping when Mr. and Mrs. Darcy walked down the aisle, now man and wife.

I was not in love with Fitzwilliam!

But nor did I want to see him marry a woman who was not good enough for him.

Yet now, I just had.

And again, he would remember this as the happiest day of his life.

# Chapter Nineteen

## HERTFORDSHIRE

Naturally, it was not fitting to remain with them on their marriage weekend, so Fitz paid for a hotel room for me that was in Mayfair. I was a little happy to be away, for the last thing that I wanted was to be there with them at such a time.

Therefore, while alone, I took some of my remaining money that Fitz had given me that I hadn't spent yet and visited King's Cross, which I liked immensely for its non-touristy feel.

When not walking around, I spent more of my day also researching any potentiality for time travel to unfold what could have happened to me. I visited libraries, researching theories, and made quite a few friends there.

However, I soon got distracted and began to read novels more than anything else. Eventually, I perused the classics section, and I came upon a novel named *Emma*, by Jane Austen. And it was set in my own times. Quickly opening it, I felt as if I had been transported back to England, in 1812, and the feel of the country, and the luxuriousness of a nice estate, as well as the smell of woods and hills, returned. I wanted home! I did still long for it! And being unable to put this novel down, I knew that I needed to purchase it. To have and to hold. I asked the librarian where the nearest bookstore was so that I could purchase it. She informed me that I was in luck, for they were selling older books that they had an excess of on the second floor.

She offered to escort me there to help me find more novels like *Emma*. Together, we stumbled on other books written by Miss Austen. We found *Mansfield Park, Northanger Abbey, Lady Susan, Sense & Sensibility*, and *Persuasion*. The librarian said that Jane Austen had written another one, but we couldn't find it. Either way, I purchased the ones that she did give me, and I found completion with that. When reading them, I was returned to a time that I had been removed from, all felt as if it could be undone, and what was lost was found again.

When opening her books, I felt as if my parents and sisters were living within them. And with each page that I turned, they would show up, and be occupants in the village of the heroine. With every word that I read, from the dialogue in *Emma* to the depths of *Persuasion*, I felt a great internal and external unwinding. I gradually would feel as if the environment around me faded away or burnt up like pieces of paper. The cars, the subway, the skyscrapers, and the concrete jungle around me all but disappeared. Then in its place rose up roaming hills, beautiful farms, peaceful woods, and all the comforts of provincial life in a rural setting. Next, all my modern-day clothing fell away from my person, and was replaced with a petticoat, comfortable boots, muslin gowns, and a shawl. And the light footsteps of family were heard behind me as I fell back onto a chair in Longbourn. Here, within the pages of *Sense & Sensibility*, time had been reversed, and I was home again.

However, eventually, I would have to put the book down, and 21$^{st}$ century England would return around me and I was still wearing sweatpants and a t-shirt with the word 'Hufflepuff' written on it.

Sadness should have overtaken me each time this occurred, yet it didn't. For that is the true magic of a book, a piece of art, a sport, or any recreation that finds you—it becomes light. A great novel loves anyone who opens it! And when all else feels as if the darkness is descending, the book becomes a refuge—a sanctuary, a pocket galaxy that is tucked away from the cold galaxy that it is within. A great novel is a beacon of light. It's that one light of happiness that shall never fade, never be touched, or altered—it is a light that shall always be there, when all other lights go out.

But time travel! That also was never far from my thoughts. So, I continued to look things up on the computers, always wishing to find more, but it always felt so inconclusive, because there was no known theory, and only speculation. Time travel was said to be something of another dimension, where it was something that could be traveled through, but there were no known equations, no machines that ever worked. It was only something that remained in the realm of the fictional and no more.

Out of curiosity though, one day, I searched the internet, typing in the word Longbourn Estate, and to my surprise, one article came up saying:

**Longbourn, Hertfordshire: an 18<sup>th</sup> century house preserved to this very day.**

I clicked on it and then read the description.

*Longbourn has a long history and is one of the few houses in Hertfordshire that is an exact model of the 18<sup>th</sup> century English architecture for rural homes of the country gentry. For the last two hundred years, it has been owned by the family Collins, who still hold residence there but allow planned and paid visits from tourists to the Hertfordshire countryside.*

When I read this, I blinked, quite frozen and not knowing how to react.

Longbourn was now owned by the Collins family! But how could that be?

Unless…

But no!

Yes, it had to be the only way. Or perhaps it could have happened later, after my sisters, but if it was not so, then this was a frightening revelation. Could it be?

Could it be that Mr. Collins, our cousin, who due to the entail, was to inherit Longbourn, did in fact inherit it? Of course he would have. It was only a matter of time, I suppose, and I, like my sisters, was simply in denial about the reality that our mother always kept pressing upon us to recall.

I suppose, in that moment, her worrying did in fact feel quite justified. After all, what happened to my sisters? Did they have a home when my father passed away? Were they able to get married? And if not, did my uncles and aunts, the Phillips and the Gardiners, take them in? How degrading for my mother that would have been, to go from being a mistress of a house to being the guest and no more.

I drummed my hand against the desk and decided not to worry over it any longer. It was too late to change anything, so worrying would affect nothing. Besides, I still didn't even know what had fully happened, therefore, perhaps all had to turn out right in the end for them.

Perhaps Jane did fall in love and married a rich man, and hopefully Lydia didn't shame our family completely at some point in time. And if so, hopefully Kitty didn't follow in her footsteps. Oh dear, I truly did miss them all at that moment.

How much I now could not wait till Fitz was to take me there, for even if I had mastered driving, I couldn't achieve it all by myself.

While the days rolled onward, I began to resign myself to the fact that I had no choice; I was to remain in that time period of London, so I had to, as the phrase put it, 'keep buggering on'.

Caroline had mentioned nanny and babysitting agencies set up in town, so I looked them up and found some that she had already mentioned. Unfortunately, I had no prior history to speak of, or job experience, so I was a little intimidated to create a profile and to arrange for any sort of interview.

Yet, by the end of two weeks' time, Caroline's brief reprieve from her post at the magazine called her away again, and Fitz was able to see me rather than just send me random messages through the email he set up with me. When he came to the hotel to meet me and take me out to a café, he rose out of his car, tall, handsome and looking quite relaxed.

"How does married life suit you?" I smiled, despite not wishing to mention it. "For you look happy."

"In truth, when you're with a woman as long as I have been with Caroline," he noted, "technically you were already married. The ceremony just made it official."

"But to have done the deed…"

"Ah, to have done the deed," he repeated.

When seeing him approaching me, I felt quite overpowered and I wished to do as I always did with him and confess to him all—as I always had the unfortunate impulse to do.

"I missed you," I admitted quite simply.

"Did you?" he asked, stopping when he neared me.

"Yes. It just occurred to me that this was the longest we have ever been away from each other for quite some time."

"Well, I do not deny that it was quite strange not having you raiding our refrigerator and always having to get you acquainted with every television show that I love. Yes, I do believe that I have gotten quite used to it."

"Well, I gave you no choice really."

"No," he agreed, "you did not. Sorry that I had to be away."

"But you had a wife to make happy."

"Precisely. But how have you been, Elizabeth? Really."

"I've been—well, Fitz, to be honest, I feel quite confused."

"About what?"

"I've been trying to apply for babysitting and nanny jobs through agencies, but it has been made clear to me that I lack the experience to get any such post, and any interviewer would fling me out of the door soon after I had applied. I don't even have a resume."

"Would you like me to make some calls?"

"Oh, but you've done so much already," I demurred.

"I've given you a few fishes every now and again. Give a man a fish, you feed him for a day, but you teach him to fish, and you feed him for life."

"Ah, I've heard that saying before."

"Yes, and it speaks true now. Do you really think you can be a good babysitter and nanny?"

"I've looked after children many times before and I also am willing to clean a house when the parents are away."

"You promise?"

"I promise."

"Then I'll call this one company that Caroline mentioned. I think she is growing more used to the idea of you, by the way."

"Good," I said, not believing it for a second. "Because I really do come in peace." I raised my hands in a mock sort of surrender and supplication.

His eyes were warm as he looked at me. "I know you do now. So, I also came to arrange for our trip."

My heart leapt in my chest. "You really still wish to take me into Hertfordshire?"

"Yes, I promised, didn't I?"

"Yes, you did. But now I am afraid. I looked it up. Longbourn still does exist."

"Yes, it does, but isn't that a good thing?"

"It's owned by a family called the Collins. That means there is a chance, that in my time, our cousin, Mr. Collins, did inherit the estate. Oh, Fitz, what if he kicked my sisters and mother out of it?"

"Oh." He pondered the question.

"Yes, and it scares me to learn the truth."

"Well, I know that it's hard for you because it felt like it was only a few months ago, but in all honesty, it's been over two hundred years, and I believe that they must have found a way to recover and keep going. And that didn't offer much comfort really, did it?"

"Not really, but thanks for trying."

"Yeah, I'm a wee bit rubbish at this whole condolence thing, huh."

"Oh, not total rubbish," I assured him.

"But rubbish enough. Well, don't worry until you know for a fact that something bad did occur. I wanted to know if you really still do want to go to Hertfordshire, because we can plan a visit to tour the estate today, if you like."

"Oh, I very much would love to do it still."

"Good."

"But Fitz, I must warn you. There is still most likely that we shall never discover what happened to the Mr. Fitzwilliam Darcy from your past."

"I know, but I am resigned to that."

"I am sorry."

"It's not your fault."

❦

Fitz and I planned the trip and very soon we were able to leave for Hertfordshire early in the morning, and then after a while, we arrived in my home county which looked a vast deal different than how it was in my day.

There was a hill and a collection of trees there that looked similar but change and time had its powerful effect and Hertfordshire felt quite modernized. Inside, it made me quite sad.

And then we neared my home as we rode along a paved street, then we turned down a lane and there, ahead of me, was the familiar sight.

"Longbourn!" I gasped, quite overwhelmed.

"How does it look compared to what you remember?" Fitz asked as we drove toward it.

"The same," I cried. "Oh, Fitzwilliam, it looks the exact same!"

And it did. From the outside, Longbourn was still as Longbourn ever was, and for one moment, one brief moment, I expected my sisters and parents to emerge from it and rush to meet me. And perhaps they would! Perhaps they had fallen through time like I had and were just waiting for me on the other side of the door.

After all, it was clear that time would be confused, mixed up—and time could be unwritten, then rewritten. I was proof of that.

Yet it also gave me hope. Such a fleeting hope. For after all that I had discovered in the world, after all the change, birth, and death of many things, all that had risen and fallen, but to see my home there—to see how after everything had given way to time, Longbourn would still be there! Yes, it gave me a great deal of hope indeed.

Eventually we parked, emerged from the car, approached the front door, Fitz knocked, and I heard footsteps.

Would it be Hill? Our servant.

Or Jenny perhaps.

Or perhaps Jane or Kitty would be curious and answer it themselves, with Lydia rushing up behind them.

The door opened, and my mouth dropped open.

And only to be closed the second afterwards when I suffered the disappointment of seeing a face that I did not know.

It was the owner of the house, named Mr. Henry Collins, who had been expecting us. He allowed us to enter, informed us that the rest of the family had been away at the time and we had the house all to ourselves.

He began to lead us around, from room to room, and secretly I wanted to throttle him.

He was showing me around my home! Of course he did not know that, but still it didn't make his appearance any less vexing to my very core. I lived there long before he did, yet I calmly allowed him to show us the rooms.

Yet as I had felt elation when I first approached my house and saw how the house had not changed, it very soon evaporated when I saw how much the interior had altered. Yes, the house itself had the same structure, but the kitchen was changed to a modern one, the dining room and parlors were luckily the same, however. I recalled how no more than five months ago, I was sitting with Jane on the one couch that was in the corner, and we were sewing something that was of little use and no beauty. Indeed, she and I were actually not the best at sewing something, even with samplers.

We also went upstairs and were shown into a bedroom that actually was preserved. When we entered it, I gasped.

"My room!" I cried, much to the surprise of Fitz and the confusion of Mr. Collins.

"Sorry," Mr. Collins said, "but what did you say?"

"Oh, I'm so sorry," I rushed out, eager to hide my mistake. "It is just, this room greatly reminds me of my old bedroom when I was growing up."

"Oh, yes, did you grow up in a house similar to this one?" he asked.

"Indeed, I did."

"No one uses this room ever, because we want there to be one bedroom that is fully preserved from the Georgian Era."

"Very good of you. In the Georgian Era, you are referring to early 19th century, aren't you? Around the time of The War of 1812, am I correct?"

"Yes, I believe so."

"Then, if I have done my research correctly, this room belonged to one of the five Bennet sisters."

"Ah, yes it was. And by that, you mean the last five Bennet sisters who lived here before my ancestor took it over."

"Yes," I replied, flinching slightly, "and what happened to the family that lost the home?"

"Well, there was an entailment, in that time, where the house was passed down through the male line. Since that generation of the Bennets had no sons in the family, but five daughters, when the late Mr. Bennet passed away, Longbourn was handed to my ancestor, Mr. William Collins."

"Well, that was fortunate for him," Fitz inserted, "but tell me, what happened to the five sisters and the mother?"

"That's the curious thing," Mr. Collins said, scratching his head. "We have always been a little curious about that, because we know that William Collins married a woman who was a resident of Hertfordshire, but it wasn't one of the sisters. So we did some digging, but interestingly enough, or should I say, disappointingly enough, the trail disappears."

"What do you mean?" I asked. "I'm sorry, but I am afraid that I do not understand."

"It's as if, all trace of the sisters just evaporates once they leave Longbourn. We have no records of them once they leave, where they went and if they stayed with family or found their own lodgings. And my ancestor, well, it is as if he didn't even want much of a record of them."

When I heard this, I felt my resolve slipping and I felt Fitz's eyes upon me. Yet I knew that I had to maintain my composure, so I just tapped my thigh nervously and continued to keep a brave face.

"You said that your ancestor, Mr. William Collins, married a local resident. Who was the lucky lady?"

"Oh, thank goodness that I thought to check this before you came, because I often forget the name. She lived nearby at an estate called Lucas Lodge."

"Lucas Lodge?!"

"Yes, her maiden name was Charlotte Lucas."

⁂

"Charlotte!" I exclaimed on the ride back away from Hertfordshire. Soon after we had learned that there was nothing of use that I could glean about my family from Mr. Henry Collins, we toured the rest of the house and then departed.

"Did you know the woman?" Fitz asked as we drove away from Longbourn.

"Yes," I hissed. "She and I were close friends."

"Were you?"

"Yes, we were."

"Some close friend she was," he jabbed, "to marry the man who was to inherit your house and be responsible for kicking your family out of their home."

"I know!" I cried, feeling utterly betrayed. "I never would have believed her capable of that."

"No loyalty when it comes to matters of competition over the heart, that's what it goes to show you."

"Maybe she had different expectations," I surmised, trying to find reasons behind her choice. "Maybe she thought that if she married him, she could convince him to let us all stay there."

"You can tell yourself that, if it gives you comfort."

"You are determined to think more ill of her than I."

"Well, forgive me for being cynical, but that's just my way. And believe me, if she married him, she did it mostly for her gain than for any consideration for you and your family. When people get married, they do it for themselves and for no one else. I would know, I married for the sake of my own happiness, as I had the right to. The difference is that I didn't, nor wouldn't, marry a woman who was to inherit my best mate's home. Simply put, there are things one should never do. Yet, I have never met her, so I do not know her as you do."

"You do not, but your points are valid, and you are speaking objectively and perhaps correctly. If I ever get back, I shall have to watch things most acutely. I wish rather than expect you to be in error. But I know that you speak from a more rational viewpoint than I do in this instance."

He took his gaze off the road briefly and turned to me. "You still believe that you might return?"

"Before now, I simply did not know, but now, knowing what I do, I hope that I do return. Oh, Fitzwilliam, you don't know what it felt like. When we rode up, all felt the same because it looked the same. Yet when I entered, and I saw how that was not the case, I felt as if I had walked into a dream that turned into a nightmare.

"Longbourn was no longer Longbourn, and it hurt. Thank goodness that we weren't in the presence of that Mr. Collins for long as well, and I was happy that we left soon, because being near him antagonized me. He was kind, and it wasn't his fault, I know, but just —I didn't want to be near him anymore."

"Right."

I turned to Mr. Darcy and immediately felt humbled by his silence.

"Oh, forgive me, I must sound like a whining brat right now."

"No, you just sound heartbroken."

"Because I am, I guess."

He briefly patted my hand. "It's fine. We all have to be heartbroken sometimes, I suppose."

"Do you ever wish that we did not have to ever be?"

"Oh, Elizabeth, many times. I am sorry that you didn't find any answers."

"And I'm sorry that you didn't either. And we still don't know anything about the other Mr. Darcy."

"I suppose there is another thing that we have to add to our list of things that we would rather not undergo."

I slanted him a glance. "And what is that?"

"Disappointment."

"Ah, yes! Yes, that is a very good word for the moment, isn't it?"

"Yes, it is."

I turned away from him and looked out of the window.

How heartbroken I was now.

And how lost.

Fitz had gotten no answers.

I took him all that way, and he had gotten no answers.

I disappointed him.

And I also disappointed myself.

Why he wasn't upset with me, I know not, for I did quite lead him down a wild goose chase.

As we drove along, I looked out at the landscape of Hertfordshire as it rolled on.

All had changed.

And all was going to change.

Including Longbourn.

For the first time, there truly did feel like an end to the dream. Yes, I wanted to return home, I wanted to know if my family was safe, but it was beginning to appear more and more as if there was no going back.

My will was set, yes, but I lacked the means.

The rolling scenery eventually had a soporific effect on me as I felt my eyelids grow heavy, and then, despite all my best efforts to remain awake, my eyes closed, and I gave in to the comforts of slumber.

# Chapter Twenty

## DERBYSHIRE

We returned to London where Fitz had me check out of the hotel and return back to Caroline's home. He informed me that she would not be at home very often, for she had to travel a great deal due to her magazine issues, deadlines, and fashion shows. He was going to join her in a few weeks' time for some show premiere, which I knew that I would not be proper to attend it.

Yet with her being away, I would not feel as if I was being such a terrible imposition again. This once more made me wonder why, in the name of Shakespeare(!), Caroline was so erratic—and clearly a little mental. She was wary of me developing any sort of attachment to Fitz, but she would leave him on a whim and he would be left to his own devices. Perhaps she did try to bully him however into not seeing me, and Fitz, in his solid stubbornness, simply stood his ground. Either way, I was happy for the arrangement, especially since the hotel bill was increasing.

Yet our days of peaceful domestic co-existence was not to last for long. Three days after we returned from Longbourn, Fitz's job called him away to visit a client who wished to meet him in person to advertise some holiday cottages that the realtor built for people to use as vacation rentals. He wanted Mr. Darcy to come himself, inspect the cottages and develop a campaign and slogan, and Mr. Darcy had accepted the plan. Yet when he came to approach me on the matter, it was a welcome surprise, for we were to head out to the country— country indeed.

"Elizabeth," he said, after he had spoken with the client, "I have to head out for a few days, so you don't mind being dragged along, do you?"

"Not at all," I agreed happily. "But only if it has the chance to be an adventure."

"It's out in the country."

"Ah, what country are we to go to?"

"The client had built cottages in my home county. We're going to Derbyshire."

❦

When Fitz told me this, I was quite excited and asked him if we would therefore have to stay at Pemberly. He confirmed that we would, I was happy about it, and therefore felt as if I now had something else to look forward to.

When the day came for our trip, I was happy to be gone since it had rained in London for three days straight, and even though the country could always boast of the same monotony of weather, at least I would get to see the estate of the man he descended from almost two hundred years before.

"I've phoned ahead," Fitz said, "and told the housekeeper to hire some maids to help get the place tidy and prepared for us to come."

"Ah, the removing of the cloth and covers from all the furniture, huh?" I suggested. "So, when was the last time that you visited Pemberly?"

"I don't know actually. There haven't been many tourists visiting it this past year, so I had no reason to check the maintenance of it, and I do believe that I haven't been there since last January."

"This business deal must be pretty important to lure you back there," I acknowledged.

"Oh, it is. If I land this deal, it would secure the company for another decade, because this will be a never-ending advertisement. The realtor built cottages for people who want to visit Derbyshire, and can rent them instead of remaining in hotels. It would be a popular concept, and we could advertise it well."

"Don't feel as if you have to entertain me while being there," I counseled him, "I am fond of walking and am just as interested in looking at the countryside as anything else."

"Good, because Pemberly has a lot of land around it."

"I've heard that it does. And I look forward to seeing it."

"You really are excited simply over hills and woods, aren't you?"

"Of course, you prat, after all, it's not like we have 'Doctor Who' and 'Downtown Abbey' in 1812, you know. A girl has to find pleasure where she can."

"Besides your family, do you miss anything about Georgian England?"

"Well, of course I... I'm sure that I miss some of the—one of the..." I trailed off when I realized that Fitz had been right all along. "Oh dear, I don't think that I miss anything besides my family. I mean, in this time, we wouldn't have to worry about an entail. And even if so, we can work and provide for ourselves if need be."

With a nod, he answered, "Yup, I knew that would happen."

"And this era is easier to survive."

"Is it? I never would have thought that."

"Oh believe me, Fitz, if you were to have been the one to fall into my time, you would not have endured more than a week before you pulled out all your hair with frustration."

"Well, I am impatient about things."

"So am I, very much."

To Derbyshire we went, and as we traveled into the countryside, I felt a welcome change, similar to how I had felt when I first saw London and when I had first got to walk around Philadelphia.

How ironic it was that I felt more comfortable in America than I had felt in my own home county of Hertfordshire. Yet I suppose that it had been because I had no expectations of Philadelphia, therefore I was able to enjoy it and learn to love it. One can always enjoy something when the emotional desire to be satisfied by it is not there.

Yet when it had come to Hertfordshire, I had such high hopes for it to fold its arms around me and return me to the way things were—to the moments of my past, but it was not to be so. I was from Hertfordshire—but it, as I once knew it was long gone, and therefore I found that I could never go back there. However, when coming to Derbyshire, because I had nothing but my curiosity attached to it, like when I was in Philadelphia, I was able to see all with admiration.

"Ah, here we are now," Fitz said as we were riding along a road that was surrounded by trees that framed the road very well. "Once we reach the end of this road, you'll get a clear look at Pemberly at a short distance."

"Right."

Eventually we made it through the trees, and up ahead, there was Pemberly itself, and Fitz slowed down his car.

"Well, there she is. Pemberly herself. What do you think of her?"

I could not speak at first, for the house was so perfect, almost too perfect from the distance that we saw it as it was framed so well against the grounds. A lake in front of it had the house's reflection in it. My mouth dropped open and now I learned everything. Back home, in 1812, when Mr. Bingley came to Hertfordshire, and he brought Mr. Darcy with him, between the two, Mr. Darcy perhaps was the true big catch. The alpha and the omega of romantic desires and pursuits. Such a home was perfect now, but then—it would have felt like the greatest thing in the world, the loveliest house in all of Britain.

"Well now." I sighed, turned to Fitz. "And this is what you stay away from. How do you do it? You have the greatest home I have ever seen."

"I stay away because such a large house is too big for me."

"You don't think your personality large enough to fit it?" I joked.

"Yes, that is precisely it."

My smile faded when he confessed this.

"Oh, forgive me, I didn't know that I would be correct about that."

"Yes, well, you were."

"Do you want to talk about it?" I asked him delicately.

Fitz shrugged and then dismissed his true feelings, masking it behind his stoic expression.

"Nah! No need to care about that, because right now, let me just take you to the house."

He drove up to the house, parked and the house looked even more incredible up close. Once we got out, I jumped out of the car and twirled around.

"Oh, Fitz, watch me as I twirl around your grounds!"

"You are so nonsensical sometimes," he joked.

"We humans are all a little bit mad," I declared, "therefore why delay the inevitable? It seems healthier to admit it. You've brought me to Pemberly!"

"Yes, and you clearly like it!"

"Of course I do!"

We both got our bags from the car and then Fitz took out his key and opened the door. As we entered, we very quickly were met by the housekeeper, Mr. Reynolds, who was kind, attentive, was very open with me, and I liked him immediately. He had our bags brought to our rooms, Fitz told him where he wished for me to sleep and all he asked at first was some tea and biscuits.

We sat down for a time in one of the smaller sitting rooms, and Fitz allowed me to take my shoes off to get more comfortable. He assured me that Mr. Reynolds would be willing to join me if I ever wished to walk around the grounds with a guide to get a history of the land. However, Fitz himself insisted on telling me the history of the rooms and giving me a grand tour. For he was actually taught the known history of much of the estate, dating back to the Victorian Era, but not much about before that.

"One of Queen Victoria's children actually was friends with one of us Darcys," he told me, "and they stayed here for a time on holiday."

"Really? That's brilliant. Wouldn't it have been funny if they had tea and biscuits like we are now?"

"I wouldn't be surprised if they did. Tea and biscuits are timeless."

Once we had rested, Fitz stood up and then offered the tour of the best parts of the house. I was eager to see much and possessed a lot of energy. Therefore, as he showed me around, there was even more to admire from within as from without. When we reached a long hallway, I began to twirl and skip down the hall.

"Did you really grow up here?" I asked as I danced.

"Yes, I did," he replied, just watching me as I giddily skipped about.

"A city boy at heart raised here, but really Fitz, this home is so lovely, that I daresay no one would disapprove of it. But if your heart is not here with it, then that is fine too."

"Oh, so you now accept that there is more to me besides this fancy house," he answered with a chuckle.

"I always knew there was, you large rock. Yet, I like it still. In truth this house has quite cooled or helped me forget my disappointment at Longbourn."

"And how it's no longer your home? Yes, I noticed that."

"And you were right to, for it's what I felt. Yet this house, well, I feel like it is similar to how it always was."

"Oh yes, we did our best to preserve it and maintain the Regency style of it."

"Precisely. I feel as if the past is here. And it helps me feel as if, as if, well as if, I am not alone. Does that sound quite mad?"

"Yes, you do sound mental right now."

"Ah, cheeky fellow!"

"So, have I shown you enough of the house for one day? Or are you still thirsty to see the whole thing?"

"If you wouldn't mind showing me all of it, then I would like it, unless you won't."

"I think I can manage it."

Fitz showed me everything, giving me details about when furniture was purchased by the family and what era it came from. By the time he finished, the cook that Mr. Reynolds hired for us had made us a meal, and we sat down to dinner.

It was cut short however because Fitz promised Caroline that he would speak to her through Skype messaging at a certain time, so I retired in my room, but I was content nonetheless.

❧❧

The next day Fitz met with the realtor of the cottages, and despite his initial impulse to leave me at the estate so that I wouldn't get bored, he found that it would help if I did attend. He deduced that it always helped a business transaction to have company with them, especially if that company was a young woman who seemed to be a friend.

We met the realtor, he showed us the cottages, which I liked and complimented, and this gave the man courage to pitch his proposal and desires to Fitz, who was altogether amenable to the business. It seemed to end in success, so when we returned to Pemberly, Fitz had offered him their marketing services, and would offer them a serviceable payment plan.

This news had him return to Pemberly in good spirits, and while I did not do much, I felt that I had contributed well enough simply by being supportive in the scheme.

Upon our arrival back to the great estate, Mr. Reynolds met us and asked Fitz if he wished to keep the ballroom closed off, or if he wished to inspect it.

"A ballroom?" I asked. "You have a ballroom as well?"

"Well, yes," he answered, "Pemberly had hosted many balls in its day."

"Oh, I should not be surprised. What does it look like?"

Mr. Reynolds chimed in. "Ah, something tells me that your guest wishes to see it, sir."

"Don't worry, Mr. Reynolds," Fitz said, "you can relax, sir, and I shall show her it myself."

He got the key from Mr. Reynolds and we traveled to the ballroom.

"You had a ballroom and you were going to conceal it from me," I teased. "What a devilish impulse, sir."

"It came from no devilish impulse this time, I can assure you. I just merely forgot."

"Ah, never think that a man would consider a ballroom to be of import." I spoke teasingly.

"And of course think of a woman to value it," he vollied.

"Yes, the difference of the sexes."

We reach a large set of doors, Fitz unlocked it and then we entered a large hall that clearly was fashioned for the exact purpose for ballroom dancing. As we entered, we both looked on everything and I was not alone in my wonder.

"I haven't been in here since I was a child," he said, "and I remember thinking the room was so big that it quite baffled me. I didn't like being in the room, you could guess, because it made me feel so small."

"I take it that you never danced in it."

"Well, the last ball that took place here was in 1954, I believe. And I wasn't born then."

"Well, that is the thing about ballrooms," I commented, stepping away from him and beginning to do a dance step. "They can be intimidating things, where the woman wonders if she shall be asked to dance, or will she be quite forgotten.

"And the man stands in a corner, for fear that if he asks a woman to dance, she shall reject him. Then there is that fleeting hope that here, in a ballroom, you shall meet the man who you one day perhaps may fall in love with. And then he shall look on you, he shall find you to be the most beautiful girl in the world, and then he shall be enthralled. Your hands will touch, and on the dance floor, you shall feel connected."

Wrapped up in my own memories, I continued to dance on and on, my feet recalling one of our most popular dances with ease, and all around me, I envisioned couples from our assemblies in Meryton dancing around me while I had a silent and invisible partner.

Sadly, it took me thirty seconds too long to recall that I was not alone in the room. I turned to Fitz, who was watching me in earnest, my cheeks reddened, and I stopped immediately.

"Oh, dear lord, how did I look just now?"

"Well, I've called you mental enough times for you to be used to it by now, but you really don't have to stop. You actually looked quite lovely, so go ahead, and keep dancing. I was fine with watching."

"I shouldn't, for one doesn't dance alone and have a gentleman watch her."

Acting on an impulse, I went to him and offered him my hand.

"Might I have this next dance, then?" I asked.

"Now you mock me, because you know that I don't know the dances from that time."

"They are very simple, and I can teach you as we go, don't worry. Besides, I know a nice slow one."

"I don't like to dance. Dancing is rubbish." He was clearly uncomfortable.

"You liked seeing me dance."

"Well, you were all right at it. I won't be."

"Honestly Fitz, you are the oddest fellow! One moment you are the strongest and most confident man in the world. Then in the next moment, you are afraid of many things and are quite insecure."

"I suppose that I am complicated."

"Well, I shall give you this. You've taught me that not all men are the same, for I used to believe otherwise."

He paused to answer. "We are simple, but we also are not at all at the same time."

"Well, no one is watching, so you won't have to worry about embarrassing yourself. Truly, come on, what do you have to lose?"

"Well…"

"Well what?"

"Elizabeth, you might laugh at me."

When he said that, he looked so vulnerable, so sincere, that for a moment, I was moved.

"If I laugh, it's only ever to make you comfortable. But if it is not what you need right now, then I promise that I shall not laugh at all. I will be kind. Cross my heart." I made the motion over my chest.

He bit his lip, I offered him my hand once more and then I led him to the center of the floor. I offered him instructions as he began to mimic my steps and then he steadily grew more comfortable as I encouraged him onward.

"See?" I declared, "you are doing it splendidly."

"Well… I guess I am."

"That's where you are supposed to say thank you."

"Oh yes, thank you."

"You are very welcome."

We danced on and on, and Fitz was very much a quick learner, and to my surprise, when he finished one set, he asked me to teach him another one. I did so, and as I instructed him on the movements, I got lost in the dance as well and looked on him with happiness and joy.

And it was as if I was truly seeing him for the very first time. He was handsome, I had always known this, but this was different. It was as if I had never fully taken in his beauty before. And his movements were strong but gentle all at once. His voice was deep, melodious and firm. He had a wickedness to him that made conversation light and breezy sometimes while other moments he could be grave and deep. There was a weight to his personality that brought sincerity to him often. Yet above all, he was fearless of the truth of things sometimes, even when that thing was so maddening, so eccentric, and so unbelievable. I recalled when we first met, and how he did not remain in denial once the truth was presented to him. Yet now I was seeing him as he was, and my heart skipped a beat when our hands touched. I felt breathless, exhilarated.

No, it could not be.

Caroline could not have been right!

No, I could not be falling in love with Fitzwilliam Darcy.

As the second dance came to an end, we both announced that we were tired, which gave me time to excuse myself and go to my room, which I was glad over, for I did not want to be in his presence at the moment.

Indeed, I could not trust myself.

Once I was alone in my room, I paced back and forth, disturbed about what had happened. I told myself that it was the dance that had affected me so, and had played a trick with my heart, making me feel what was not meant to be felt, but I wondered at the reverse in the next moment.

After all, how many times had I felt that Caroline was not good enough for him? Yet she was not, and I simply was aware of that. Or maybe I refused to see it because, deep down, I didn't want to admit it to myself, but she was correct. I didn't want to see any growing feelings for him, so I chose not to. Now I had gotten too far ahead of myself and there was nothing else to be done. I sat down and decided to let time tell me how I felt.

Ah, time! That polarizing and antagonizing thing.

After a couple of hours, I calmed my nerves and sudden emotions, then I walked down the steps to look for him. Eventually I crossed paths with Mr. Reynolds who informed me that he was sitting in the first parlor.

As I entered the parlor, I stifled my laughter when I found Fitz fast asleep on the couch, one leg sprawled out on it, one arm on his chest holding a book and the other arm leaning over the edge of the cushion and he looked so simple and innocent there. I tiptoed forward, to look at his face, and my heart soared slightly when I noticed that resting open on his chest was the copy of 'The Hobbit' that I had brought for him.

He clearly had gotten a quarter of the way into the book, and I wondered if I ought to remove it from his chest and place it on the coffee table, but instead I had a better notion. I went to the kitchens, asked them if they could give me a small plate of biscuits and a cup of milk and I took it to the parlor. Tiptoeing up to Fitz once more, I placed the milk and biscuits on the table gently for when he woke up, and then I began to sneak out again. Unfortunately, I scuffed my foot against the ground and then I groaned inwardly as I heard him shift on the couch.

"Elizabeth?" he called sleepily. I turned around slowly and saw that he was rubbing his eyes.

"Hello," I spoke. "I saw you resting, so I was going to leave you alone."

"Ah, well then…" then he noticed the milk and cookies. "Did Mr. Reynolds bring me these?"

"No, I thought you might be hungry when you woke up."

"Really?"

"Yes."

Fitz took a bite of a biscuit and drank some milk.

"Yes, well, thanks a lot."

"You're welcome."

"You found me asleep after enjoying the good book you happened to have given me."

"Is it as good as you remember it?"

"Nostalgia is a great and powerful thing. So yes, I do still love it. It takes me back to my childhood, you see. And those were simpler times."

"Better times?"

"Of course," he added with a chuckle, "now sit down and have the biscuits with me."

"Don't order me around," I joked, then I sat down with him and we began to eat while just looking ahead, at the house.

"Things are always so much simpler when you're a kid, if your parents are good, which mine were. And I was good at making friends when I was a child."

I nibbled the biscuit. "When did that change again?"

"Yeah, I turned 13 and being a teenager was not the best thing for me. I've been insecure ever since."

"It's not your fault. It's a trying age."

He finished the milk. "That I thought I would overcome, but I didn't."

"We never fully do, I can imagine. I suppose that we are meant to always be wondering who the devil we are, even long after we reached that age where we expected that we would have all the answers."

"Precisely," he agreed, looking on me generously.

As he did so, his features so relaxed and his eyes so gentle, I felt such an inner disquiet, for he was so lovely—so perfect. And how I wish that I didn't see it that way. For now, everything was so very complicated.

"Is that why you would never wish to live for long here at Pemberly?" I asked gently. "And I know you don't want to talk about it, but perhaps you ought to."

"I suppose that is part of it. I do not think I have the skills to run a household, but that's not just it."

"Then what is it? Go on, spit it out. I've had you dancing earlier today, so what could you ever have to lose?"

"I suppose it is simple. Elizabeth, look at this house. Just look at it. It's huge, and to live here ever, well, I would be reminded of all these empty rooms here, and they are not filled by anyone."

"You are married now, and you might have children," I reminded him.

"Yes, we will, but still, it just feels like there is too much emptiness here and I don't know what to do with it. As if every room is an empty space that can't be filled. It's just—the place only reminds me that my parents are gone, you know, and so the place feels…"

"Empty."

"Yes."

"In ways that you can't fill up."

"Yes."

"I know the feeling. When I went to Longbourn and saw that my family was not there, and nor was their past allowed to be, I felt empty and hollow. And then it occurred to me just how much Longbourn was my family. It wasn't just the brick and the rooms, but it was them always. Longbourn was the Bennets."

"As Pemberly is the Darcys'. And there are no more Darcys left but me."

"And no more Bennets left but me."

"Our situation is perhaps the same."

"It is, except for one thing," I reminded him.

"What would that be?"

"Well, I'm a ghost to you."

He cocked his head. "What do you mean?"

"I've given this some thought. And technically speaking, yes I am here, but I'm also not. I am Elizabeth Bennet, of Longbourn, born in 1786, and therefore, if time had been linear, I would be dead now. I'm a ghost. I'm here, but I'm not here. Therefore, what must I be in your eyes?"

"You're not a ghost, Elizabeth. You're right here."

He raised his hand and was about to press it on my face and my breath stopped.

But nothing happened.

As I suppose, nothing ought to have.

Fitz stopped before he touched me and then he rested his hand on his lap. Then he stood up, turned away, walked to the window, and stared out of it.

"You're not a ghost to me," he said once more. "You are here."

"Forgive me, I was being depressing."

He turned from the window briefly. "No, you had a point. But let's not think of it that way. Let's just think of ourselves not as the present and the past, as if we are two moments that are perverse and doing it all backwards. No, let's just look at it as if we are two points in history that just happened to collide into each other."

"Not as dead or alive, but just different, huh?"

He continued to look out the window. "Yes, exactly."

"Well then, yes, I do like that. Two moments of history that have just happened to have crashed into each other."

"And we did crash, didn't we?"

I laughed, remembering the incident clearly. "Yes, we did."

I looked around the room, not knowing what else to say, then I saw the copy of 'The Hobbit' resting on the coffee table and I picked it up.

"What is this book about anyway?"

"Oh it's a fantasy. Meant for kids, but it is still enjoyable for adults. It's about this Hobbit named Bilbo Baggins. Oh, Hobbits are a race in the book who are really little and have pointy ears. They love living in holes, and... actually I am really bad at explaining it, so why don't you let me read you the first couple of pages."

"Oh, I would love that."

I handed him the book and we sat down next to each other.

"When I am finished with it," he said, "you really ought to read it yourself, for it is a classic at this point."

"Another bit of my distant future that I have to become acquainted with."

"Yes, I am quite spoiling you with all this, aren't I? I've given you so much foreknowledge, haven't I?"

"Oh nonsense," I urged. "It cannot be helped, and besides, I shall not give anyone else the idea for the book in my time, and no one would like the idea anyway, so Tolkien's book and idea will always be his own."

"True, well then, let's alternate. I'll read the first page and then you can read the second."

"Fine with me." Fitz opened the book and he began to read the first page of chapter one. His voice deep and lovely—and one simply just believed everything that he said.

"'In a hole in the ground there lived a hobbit. Not a nasty, dirty, wet hole, filled with the ends of worms and an oozy smell, nor yet a dry, bare, sandy hole with nothing in it to sit down on or to eat: it was a hobbit-hole, and that means comfort...'"

# Chapter Twenty-One

## REALITY

O ur time in Derbyshire came to a close very quickly and Fitz and I had to return to London at last. When leaving Pemberly, my soul felt a little heavy, for the feeling of fulfillment that I did not find at Longbourn, I had begun to find at Pemberly and therefore I quickly did not desire to leave it.

Yet to London we returned where Fitz applied himself to his work very quickly while Caroline was still immersed in her work. Finally I was able to get an interview at a babysitting agency, and Fitz used his influence to have landed me a job where I was a nanny for a family named Bates.

Therefore, to the happiness of the new Mrs. Darcy, I relocated to that family where I looked after the Bates two children and also cleaned the house somewhat as well when the children were at school. All the while Caroline and Fitz were quite the social couple, for I had seen them in online articles that highlighted events around the fashion and modeling scene.

They even appeared on 'Britain's Next Top Model' where Caroline oversaw one photoshoot for the television show and Fitz appeared to be the one who would market the pictures for a certain exhibit. In that time, I saw Fitz merely a little now and again, for he was kind enough to visit me. At that point, I had invested in purchasing a cell phone, for my employers required me to have one, and I would text him every now and again, but I knew it was wise to never call. He always responded and even accepted one invitation I offered of me treating him to lunch one day, in payment of all that he did for me.

Yet my time working, assisting the family that I was employed under, and always tending to the children, was both a blessing and a bane. When one grows to like someone, it hurts to see them and also to be away from them. In being away from him, I had time to gather myself, recover and compose my feelings. His appearance would not be a permanent torture for me, and Caroline would not antagonize me by being married to the first man I had ever developed such a strong attachment to.

However, being away from him came the pain of not being allowed to be in the company of the man whose good opinion I valued the most. Thus, I learned the double-edged sword of affection, and I didn't like it at all.

Yet my employers, the Bates, and their children, were a lovely family and I was fortunate, believing myself that time would heal my wound from never having hope of any kind with him. And perhaps time would do the reverse also of what wound it had inflicted before. For after two months of me remaining with the Bates family, I had resigned myself to the fact that I would never be returning home.

Longbourn was lost to me.

And Fitzwilliam Darcy was also never to be mine.

And so it was.

One day, I was walking along, the Bates children holding each of my hands. While the daughter, Gemma, was telling me about how she had almost gotten into a fight with a child at her school because he slipped a booger into her orange juice, we entered the park where they would often go and play. It was the loveliest park in the neighborhood and when we went, we were met by a few other children from the school and their parents. I found one parent who I was well acquainted with, and I asked her to look after the children for a moment while I went off and got a cup of juice for Gemma from the store across the street because she was thirsty and she of course agreed.

As I walked through the park, I began to pass a couple of trees that had quite shielded a bench somewhat and I saw two people kissing out of the corner of my eye. At first my instinct was to ignore them as I walked on, but something else overpowered that impulse, my curiosity got the better of me and I quickly glimpsed them.

And then I took another glance.

Then I stopped in my tracks and gaped at the unlikely couple.

"Caroline!" I gasped, to which she turned and looked at me, then stood up from the bench abruptly.

There was Caroline Darcy, her cheeks red from just being caught in a kiss—with a man who was not her husband!

Rather than run away quickly as I ought to have, making sure that she didn't notice me, I was quite stupid about it. Or stubborn, or stupidly brave, whatever is the term for it. One cannot predict how one would act when coming upon such a scene, so of course instinct takes over. In that moment, my instinct was only one thing: protect Fitz.

"You evil witch!" I cried, taking a step toward her and then, to the man. "And who the bloody hell are you?"

"Excuse me," he said as he stood, "you are intruding and—"

"And you're kissing my friend's wife!" I shouted. "Do you really want to test me, sir?"

When I said this, the man closed his mouth.

"Elizabeth, do shut up and let me explain!" Caroline declared, and I hated her even more after that.

"Let you explain? There is no explanation for this. Now who is he?"

"Don't worry, we're just rehearsing something."

"For what? Are you planning on doing Dinner Theatre at any time?" I scoffed. "And what? The play is called 'When My Lips Met His Mouth'. Don't make me laugh."

"No, it's for a photoshoot."

"Still, you are not much good at making me laugh, Caroline." I didn't believe her for a second. "I don't know much about your world, but kissing in a park is not a part of it, I don't believe." Then I turned back to the man. "And why are you still here?"

"Because I—"

"Oh shut it!" I shouted, and then I turned to Caroline. "Tell him to leave now."

Caroline allowed him to go and I watched him leave with animosity, before I wielded on Caroline with a fury. Yet, to my incredible shock, Caroline looked on me with wrath and resentment, and not the least bit of shame or guilt.

"How dare you come in here and speak to me in this way?" Caroline asked, "And you don't even know all the facts."

"I know that you were kissing a man in a public park like the revolting moron that you are, and you are married."

"You don't know the whole story, but even if it was what you think, it would be your fault."

"My fault?" I gasped, "how can your twisted mind come up with that?"

"You and Fitz spent so much time together, how could you not be to blame? When you did everything in your power to steal him away from me?"

"What?"

"Don't lie to me anymore. You're in love with him, and no matter what I told him, he just catered to you."

I was beyond shocked and furious. "Because he was trying to help me figure out who I was."

"While you chased after him. Admit it already, you love my husband."

"Of course I love him!" I finally admitted.

When I said this, Caroline gave me a mean look.

"But I did nothing," I continued. "I didn't even know I loved him for the longest time."

Caroline's face twisted into an unpleasant smirk. "Don't make me laugh."

"I wasn't trying to. I didn't attempt to get him, or draw him in. All I ever did was be his friend, and as much as I hated you, I never tried to take him away. Even though now I realize that I should have."

"You worthless cow!"

"Me? Look at you. You are disgusting, Caroline. You think Fitz gets distracted for a moment and you use that as an excuse to do this? You claim to love him, and you don't even know him! He would never do anything to hurt you, but you fly off the handle and get affection elsewhere. You foolish prat! I was right from the very beginning; you are not good enough for him. And you know what, you never loved him."

"I did love him! And I still do!" she insisted.

"You were kissing another man because you just wanted to. And no, you don't love him! You love the idea of him. You love what being married to him would give you. You have attention, even more money, a stable home, and more exposure to things. You get everything by being with him, but you don't care for who brings it to you. You never cared for him. You only cared for what it would do for you. And so no, you don't deserve him."

"This is coming from you? You who lied about everything when you came here."

"What?"

"I know the truth about you, Elizabeth Bennet. And I was just happy to get your disgusting and shabby self out of my house, but now you're just being a hypocrite."

"I'm being a hypocrite?" It then occurred to me that she must've learned somehow about how I had fallen through time, but I didn't see how she could equate my deception with her own. Thus this made her even more horrible in my eyes. Yet I did not wish to remain longer in her presence, for now I had to find Fitz, and it was imperative that he learn the truth.

Backing away from Caroline, I gave her a long and cruel look.

"You dare compare me to you?" I spat out.

"I was pushed to this. So that makes you worse than me," she reasoned.

"No, I'm not," I declared, "and I am glad of it."

Turning on my heel, I rushed away from her, went back through the park, found Gemma and her brother, and taking their hands, I demanded that we leave immediately. Gemma noticed that I was angry, and asked what was wrong, but I did my best to avoid the issue as I took them home.

At the Bates residence, I was quite restless, for I had to wait till I had made sure their homework was done, they ate with the family and I tucked them into bed before I could plan my trip into Mayfair. I had texted Fitz earlier to inform him that I needed to see him and that I was coming to their house to speak with him. I asked him to meet me in the front of the house, so that I did not disturb Caroline if she was there, for I did not wish to see her.

Fitz had not responded, but I still planned to go there anyway, assuming that he just didn't get my message. Once I had the children in bed, I put on my jacket, called for a taxi and then was off to go to Mayfair.

Once we arrived in front of the house, I paid the cab driver, then asked him if he could remain there until I returned. He agreed, then I went out and felt very frozen. I didn't move because I was unsure of what to do next, or how best to soften the news that I was about to tell Fitz. I couldn't knock or ring, for that would be bad, so I took out my phone again and this time, I called Fitz.

Once more, he did not pick up, but rather, the front door opened and he appeared there himself.

When I saw him, his face was like stone and I did not know how to read it, yet I had sensed that something was in fact quite off with his spirit.

"Fitz!"

"Hello, Elizabeth," he stated quite flatly.

"Forgive me for coming at this hour, but I desperately needed to tell you something."

"Yes, I know."

"You do? Then, has Caroline told you?"

"Yes, she has."

"Oh, that surprises me, but still, I think it best that we talk about it inside, please, for I wish to make sure that she has told you the full story. Forgive me, but I do not trust her."

"You don't trust her?"

"Yes," I replied, confused at how he would wonder that, and how he could still trust her as well, despite what she had done. "Of course I don't."

He continued to study me with a flat gaze. "If you can explain yourself, I suppose I can grant you that much."

This cruel remark set me back, but he moved aside, and I entered. I could therefore only suppose that he was frozen from hearing the news and therefore he was simply out of spirits, and his emotions and reactions were quite cold.

We entered the living room. He took a seat and looked at me, his gaze firm. I did not know how to begin, so I paced back and forth.

"How do you feel after you have learned this?" I asked.

"Well, I feel betrayed of course."

"I'm sure that you do. But never fear, time shall heal this wound, and while I am merely a friend, you can rely on me for a friendly ear if you ever need to talk about it. Of course I know that you very well would not wish to talk much about it, but if you do, then you may remember that I am here, as a friend."

"I beg your pardon?" He leaned forward and looked confused. "What do you mean?"

"Well, I know that she has hurt you terribly, and I know sometimes one does not wish to speak about what one feels when we are embarrassed by it. But you now know not to be afraid of confiding in me. I cannot begin to understand the mortification this all may have caused you, but I shall try, and your situation is a common one, and it's not your fault. It never was."

"She?" he asked even more confused. "And of course this is not my fault? And you know that more than any other, but what do you mean by 'she'?"

"Yes." The voice came from behind me. "Miss Bennet, what do you mean?"

I froze when I heard Caroline's voice behind me, and when I turned to her, she looked at me, her face set and her expression mean.

"Elizabeth Bennet," she continued, "I am appalled that you dare come here after what you did. You really have no shame, do you?"

"Me?" I gasped, not afraid of the situation. "You are the last person in the world who should ever think to call someone what you are, you spoiled cow."

"Elizabeth!" Fitz roared. "Do not call my wife a cow!"

I turned to him, incredulous.

"You are about to defend her. But—but, look what she did to you? Don't you care?"

"What she did to me?" he asked, looking confused, and that was when it occurred to me. We were speaking of different things, and Caroline must have told him something quite erroneous.

"Stop with the lies, Elizabeth Bennet," Caroline declared, "he knows now, so you can drop the charade."

"What!" I turned on her. "What are you referring to?"

"I'm referring to the fact that you lied about who you were," she snarled, approaching me like a hungry beast. "Pretending to be a woman who had lost her memory just so that you could wiggle your way into his life and use him for your own amusement. And all the while, you were just a lost camper."

"I beg your pardon? I have no idea what you are talking about."

"Like I said," she declared, then she pulled a newspaper from her briefcase before and thrust it at me. "I knew I had seen you before. You're not Elizabeth Bennet, but Elizabeth Dickens, the woman who was reported missing a few months ago, and whose family posted pictures of her all over the web. She disappeared when she was camping, and clearly it's because she was busy changing her identity so that she could frighteningly haunt an innocent man."

I looked at the newspaper and to my utter shock and horror, there was a picture of me, wearing clothes I had never seen before or wore before, sitting next to people I had never met in the course of my life.

"But... but..."

"Speechless, huh?" Caroline gloated. "Your lies have caught up with you."

"No," I refuted, "this is not me. I have never even met these people in my life, and I have no idea how this could even come about and—"

My gaze fell on Fitz, who stood there, still frozen, but his eyes contained a strong tint of doubt. He did not trust me, and it hurt.

"Fitzwilliam, this is not me."

"Really?" Caroline shouted. "And who would it be?"

"I don't know. Someone who looks like me, I suppose, but this is definitely not me at all."

"Oh, that's rich!"

Ignoring Caroline, I appealed to Fitz in supplication.

"You know I am not lying. I cannot explain this coincidence, but that's all it is."

"Oh and we're supposed to believe that?" Caroline continued. "You lying piece of—"

"And you cannot trust your wife, Fitz," I shouted over her, "because she is just merely trying to distract me from the task that I had of coming here to tell you that she is not faithful to you."

When I said this, Fitz's head snapped in my direction and he faltered.

"What?" Caroline gasped, looking shocked.

"Oh, let me guess, you're an actress as well," I jabbed. "Why am I not surprised? For lying clearly comes second nature to you." I turned to Fitz. "I promise you, on the soul of my family, this afternoon I was walking about the park with my two charges, and I came upon Caroline here, kissing another man and it was for no photoshoot as she claimed."

"You hideous little leech!" Caroline cried. "Are you this horrible that you would lie to attempt to cover it up? How dare you accuse me of doing something like that?"

"I accuse you because you *are* horrible like that. You have been unfaithful for god knows how long and then you did it under the excuse of being jealous of my relationship with him when he has been nothing else but faithful to you. Even when I wanted him, I still did nothing, while you entertained other men countless times perhaps."

"Did you hear that!" Caroline cried, turning to Fitz. "There, you see! I told you that she liked you, and this was all a trap. You didn't believe me but believe me now. She is a scam and a worthless little snip that lied to you like the leech that she is. You should have thrown her out when you first met her!"

I was so irate, so very resentful, that before I knew what I was doing, I rushed up to Caroline and punched her.

She fell backwards and collapsed on the couch and I didn't have time to continue my attack, because Fitz grabbed me, lifted me up and carried me out of the room.

"Elizabeth!" he cried, "stop this!"

"Horrible!" I gasped. "She is evil!"

"Don't say that!"

He continued to pull me out of the house and then put me down harshly on their porch, looking down at me with pure venom. As he did so, only then did I feel fear. Only then did I feel worry and panic, for I could see it in his eyes; he believed her.

"Fitz…"

"How could you lie to me like that?" He was livid.

"Lie? I never lied. Never."

"Elizabeth, you frighten me now, for all this time, this is what you were? You created this whole scheme just for what? To get close to me? Have you any idea how horrifying that is?"

"Oh my god, you complete…" I trailed off before I could call him an idiot. "That is not me in the picture. All we have to do is find the family and her parents will surely confirm it."

"You look exactly like her."

"I don't know why, but clearly something else is happening here, and that is not me! Don't believe that harpy in there."

"That is my wife!"

"And you married the worst woman in all of England!"

Fitz's eyes turned cold. "Get out of here and never come back!"

"But Fitz…"

"I said get out!"

Suddenly Caroline emerged from the house with her phone.

"I called the police, Elizabeth. They shall be here soon, so by all means stay if you want to be arrested!"

I looked between them and felt utterly embarrassed and let down.

"I stand by everything I say," I urged him to believe. "And do you forget so easily. You heard the clock, you woke up somewhere else."

"It was just a dream, that's all."

"No it wasn't, and you know it wasn't! Oh my god, are you really going to lie to yourself like that? You cannot be this, you can't..."

I looked at both of them and saw that I had quite lost the battle. I was not surprised by Caroline for doing this, but Fitz had quite let me down. I may have hated her, but in that moment, it was him who I was most enraged with, for it was him and him alone that I had cared for.

"I was wrong," I said at last to Fitz. "You both are perfectly matched, and you deserve each other."

I turned away, rushed down the steps, was happy to see that the cab still waited for me, so I jumped into it and we rode off.

⚜

As I sat in the back of the cab, I did my best not to weep, but I could not keep from doing so, and I looked out of the window, embarrassed beyond belief.

I had loved him, and I was so naïve about it. I should have made certain that Caroline did not know that I had seen her kissing the man and then just told Fitz so that he could discover it for himself. This way, I would still have him, but I had been rash and reckless. And now I had lost everything.

Eventually, we reached the Bates home and as I paid the cab driver, he looked up at me with sympathy.

"So, you liked another woman's mate, huh?" he asked.

"It's more than that," I urged him to believe. "And we didn't do anything and... oh god. I did like another woman's mate."

"No worries, we've all been there, haven't we? The trick is, recover, and get out of the situation as quickly as you had fallen into it."

"Right. Thanks a lot."

"No problem."

When he collected his money, he drove off.

# Chapter Twenty-Two

## THE SOUND I THOUGHT THAT I WOULD
## NEVER HEAR

The next day, I sent one more text to Fitz, urging him to believe that I had not been lying to him at all and that I had spoken true, but it did no good. The post went unanswered and then he blocked my phone altogether. Such a small and simple action had quite a grand effect and I felt so rejected, so utterly smashed about and it hurt exponentially.

Yet I had to maintain an air of amusement when it came to Gemma and her brother, and I needed the job now more than ever. But I marveled at times of how we humans can feel one thing and present another. To the Bates family, I always showed a happy face, but there was not one day, not one moment, that I could release Fitzwilliam Darcy from my mind.

To have lost his faith in me and his good opinion was a great pain, but what struck me the most was not that I lost his heart, because I never had it. No, indeed. It was the fact that I could not bear to think that he was out there, alive in the world, and thinking ill of me. Yet now, that was all that he had felt.

And all that he would ever feel.

Pain does not stop the progression of time, however, and a month after the incident, I had to pick Gemma and her brother, Arthur, up from school. As I did so, Gemma was very much inclined to go to the park once more and feed the ducks some bread that she had left over from her lunch. Since Arthur was apt to go as well, I called their mother and left a message that I was going to take them there first and then proceed to their home afterwards. I brought them some ice cream and we walked along to the park, where there were some other children as well. I took the bread and began to rip it apart for Gemma and Artie, handing it to them for them to feed the ducks as we remained right next to the pond the whole while.

As we stood there, I grew distracted for a moment when I looked at my own reflection, and my mind wondered.

What was my family doing at that moment, two hundred years ago? If only I could return there, Jane would be able to comfort me. Then again, Jane would never be allowed to know of what occurred to me, for even she would doubt my sanity.

"Oh, look, Elizabeth!" Gemma cried, "That duck there has ducklings!"

I smiled at her and doing my best to bring myself out of my despondent mood, I began to help her feed them. Indeed, it had been a month, and it was time for me to put the past experience behind me and live in the present. After all, the present was all that I had left now. And yet, I wondered what sort of future I could have? Yet it was too much to consider, for the future now appeared to be the most horrifying thing in the world. I suppose it was because I didn't know it. And I was not used to not knowing.

Yet I breathed in evenly, looking at little Gemma, and seeing her happy face, I decided that there was no point in feeling sorry for myself, because that would do me no good. No, I had to cast off the somberness and be as I once was.

As I closed my eyes, urging myself to remain strong, I wanted to kick myself when I heard Fitz's voice call my name.

I groaned. "Really Lizzy, this is what you call moving on? Seriously, embrace the feminist movement already."

And then I heard him call my name again, and it was getting ridiculous.

"Elizabeth," Gemma said, "that man is calling after you over there."

"What?" I said, coming out of my own thoughts.

"Elizabeth Bennet!"

I was not mistaken, and to my horror I turned to see Fitzwilliam Darcy a distance away, walking towards me.

◈

When first seeing him, my immediate instinct was to take the children away from him, for I had only one impulse: retreat. Therefore, I took their hands, gave Fitz one fleeting look, then I urged them to hastily come along.

"Elizabeth!" he called.

"Leave me alone!" I spat over my shoulder.

"I'm sorry!" he cried.

When hearing this, I slowed down and turned toward him.

"What did you say?" I called.

"Forgive me," he said, "I am sorry. I was wrong."

"You learned the truth then?"

"Yes, I did. Someone else discovered it and told me. I'm sorry, I should have believed you!"

"I never hurt you, believe me."

"I know. I know it now! And I'm here. I believe you. I believe everything. And please, I'm listening, so forgive me."

"You really mean it?"

"Yes, I do," he said, coming toward me. Still holding the children's hands, I walked towards him and didn't bother to see where I was walking, because I accidentally waded into the pond. Gemma and Artie laughed at this, as did the people around me, and I laughed as well.

"I guess I am happy," I said to Fitz as he continued to come forward.

"And I'm a large git," he answered with a smile.

"Yes, you are, and..."
Tick.
Tock.
Tick.
I heard a clock.
And not just any clock.
It was the clock.
Time was moving again.

When I heard it, I froze with fright. If time was moving, then so might I. As I did so, I looked on Fitz and his face was stricken with horror.

"Do you hear that as well?" I asked.

"Yes," he whispered, "yes I do."

"Yes."

"What's going to happen?"

"I think, I'm going to be..."

The clock sounds began to grow louder as I flinched from the weight of it. I felt a weight press on me, and I knew that it was happening in full, but then suddenly the impulse hit me. I was being taken, but Fitz might be left behind. So not to give the children the misfortune of following after me, I relinquished their hands, but with Fitz, I was going to be selfish, not caring for his happiness.

"Fitz!" I cried, rushing to grab him and take him with me. His instinct was the same however, and we ran to each other. Yet as we did, I saw my hand disappear before we touched, and then my legs, my body, and then my eyes closed as all faded to black.

# Chapter Twenty-Three

## THE NEW/OLD ACQUAINTANCE

M y body was wet all over; my feet were on the bottom of a stream, and then I pushed my body up, only to find that I was back in the stream in Hertfordshire.

As I roared out, in triumph and amazement about how I possibly could have returned, it took only a matter of a few seconds for me to remember myself.

"Fitzwilliam!" I cried. "Where are you?"

I looked around, attempting to wade from the stream as my sodden clothing kept slowing me down.

I looked through the trees. "Fitz, where are you?" I kept looking on and on, and the longer that I got no reply, the more forlorn I felt.

We had not touched.

And therefore, he did not follow after me.

I had left Fitzwilliam Darcy behind in 2016.

With eagerness I walked back to Longbourn, but with weight did I carry my legs. I was so happy to be returned back to my time, but I wanted to bring him back! Even if it would have been hard for him to adapt, I could teach him, I could have him! I could have a man that I loved, for the first time ever.

And now I had lost it, and once more I cursed time. It was as if I was given an ultimatum. Either I was to get Fitz, or get my family, but I could not have both. How ironic it was now, that finally as I had gotten home, my mind immediately had turned to think of a way I could journey forward in time, find Fitzwilliam and get him to come with me.

Until Longbourn came into view.

There it was, but not the Longbourn of 2016, but the Longbourn of 1812, and that was what I had needed. I looked down at myself, wearing my contemporary clothes, drenched and looking like a drowned rat, but I cared not. So I rushed forward, ran into the house and tried to go up the steps to change, unnoticed. Unfortunately, the servant Hill came upon me, and while she carried a pitcher of water, she dropped it when she glimpsed me.

"Miss Elizabeth!" she cried.

"Sorry, Hill, I know I must look affright."

"As much as you did a few minutes ago. But at least you are remembering yourself now, but where did you get those other change of clothes? And weren't you taking a bath?"

"What?" I asked, confused, "I was out at the stream and I fell in."

"Yes, three hours ago."

"I beg your pardon?"

"Yes, you came here, three hours ago, with Kitty, who had to practically drag you in here, for you had quite forgot yourself."

"What?"

I heard footsteps and from out of the sitting room, I was greeted by the shocked faces of Jane, Mary, and my mother. So happy to see them, I jumped down the steps.

"Mama!" I cried. "Jane and Mary!"

I rushed to them, and in my wet clothes, I hugged them.

"Elizabeth, dear!" our mother cried. "What has gotten into you today? First you go off for a walk, then Kitty brings you back in hysterics and you claiming that you are not who you are, then claiming that you are in the wrong year and everything! And now here you are again, in even more strange clothes?"

"Wait," I said. "I was here before?"

"Yes, Lizzy," Jane said, "when Kitty brought you in here, you were quite... bewildered."

"You believed that you were not yourself," Mary added. "It was like you forgot entirely who you were, and you were wearing a whole set of strange clothes."

"And where did you get those other strange clothes from?" My mother cried, "Dear Lizzy, you do carry on too much in wild ways. You shall be the death of me."

"Sorry mama," I said, kissing her cheek.

"And I thought I had convinced you to take a bath," Jane said, "yes, you are supposed to be in the bath now."

"Am I?" I asked, "Then excuse me."

I went up to the steps, ran to our washroom, with Jane following after me.

"Lizzy, I do not understand."

"Neither do I. Well, I suppose that it's just one of those days."

I rushed forward, went into the washroom and sure enough, there was a tub drawn and there were a pair of shoes and socks on the ground that I recognized as being converse sneakers. Suddenly it all came clear to me.

"We swapped places," I said aloud as I recalled the woman that Caroline accused me of being, the other Elizabeth. The one who looked like me. And yet, I had no idea what her connection was to me besides what we looked like, but either way, that was the only explanation. I picked up the sneakers and inspected them.

"Lizzy," Jane said, warily, "what is going on?"

"In truth, Jane," I said, "I don't know, but it doesn't matter now, because I know who I am, and I'm finally home."

Lies were the order of the day sadly, for I had to lie about why I showed up at my home twice in strange clothes, and why I forgot who

I was for a time. Wherever the other Elizabeth was, I hoped that she had returned back to 2016 and that she wasn't lost to time anywhere else. I suppose that her journey would be a mystery to me always, for I would never know why we had swapped places. Unless time would present that to me eventually.

Yet one thing was clear. We swapped places, but time had moved differently for us. She had been there for no more than a few hours. I had been in 2016 for months. Yet I had no way of accounting for why that occurred either.

Jane, Kitty, Mary and Lydia were all so very worried about me, it seemed, and when they had brought the other Elizabeth back from the stream, she had quite frightened them with her refusal to believe that she was their sister. I could very well believe it, but now I only pretended that I had knocked my head when I fell somewhere and had temporarily forgotten myself.

Yet once I was in my room, Jane helped me undress and do my hair, and it was strange, for my clothes, which had always been mine, felt so foreign to me. Yet this was quite made up for when I was sitting with my family, who had many questions, except for my father who attributed my afternoon of confusion and madness to a side effect of simply being a female.

Once I returned to my current state, Kitty and Lydia laughed it off and couldn't wait to go into Meryton and tell everyone about my episode. Mary quickly got past the occurrence and went back to her studies. My mother insisted that I ought not to go for long walks anymore, and only Jane was properly unnerved.

"You kept saying you were not yourself," she said, "and Lizzy, for one second, I believed you. I actually believed that Kitty had simply found a woman who looked just like you, but wasn't you, and that you were lost somewhere."

"Well." I smiled, sad that I could not tell her the truth. "That is actually a very wise and keen thought, but don't worry, I am here, and I won't be going anywhere or forgetting myself ever again."

Jane hugged me, content with this. Feeling her arms around me made me so very happy to be home.

ﷺ

How bitter a concept, to want to be in one place when you are at another. When in 2016, I wanted to be in 1812, and now being in 1812, I wondered what was happening in 2016. For there was one thing that Fitzwilliam was very right about; one cannot go back.

While I spent the days sitting with my family, I marveled at every moment. Every word that was spoken, every gesture and I felt an appreciation that I had not felt before. Yet for them, all was taken for granted. A moment was just another moment for them. It was the present. Whereas for me, it was a moment of the past which I almost missed and therefore I cherished it all the more. Therefore, to appreciate everything around you when no one else is noticing the things you notice, the little things, well, it does quite change things. It's as if you are living at different speeds than those around you. Yet, if it were not for the absence of Fitz, that feeling of difference would have been worth it.

I could talk of him to no one. He was only something in my memory now, a bit of the future that I would never have. Quite the bitter pill to take. For days I inwardly searched for purpose of why I was sent to 2016, and what effect I had on the era, and I could only think of one great change. Perhaps I had been sent to that time merely to save Fitzwilliam from Caroline Bingley. And I had to swap with someone who looked like me to do it. Yet, since at least I accomplished that, at least it wasn't all for nothing.

ﷺ

Of course, and not a moment too soon, the day of the Assembly came for when we would all meet Mr. Bingley and Mr. Fitzwilliam Darcy of Pemberly.

All of my sisters were looking forward to Bingley, but I could not sit still, for I was waiting for Mr. Darcy above all. I felt my spirits always roused, waiting to meet him. So on the evening of the dance, I decided to wear my finest gown and have my hair done to its very best, and with my family—except for our father, who had no desire to come, we all went into Meryton for the Assembly Room.

When we entered, Mr. Bingley's party had not arrived, and I very much wished to sit the dances out until he came. But when I was asked by a few men, I had to accept and so, it was when I was in the middle of a set with Charlotte Lucas's brother, Kenneth, that the Bingley party did eventually arrive. The dance came to an end, and I moved to the front of the group as Sir William Lucas came forward to introduce them to the room. As I moved through the crowd, my gaze fell upon the party and my jaw dropped.

"Fitzwilliam Darcy!" I gasped.

There he was—but not a different one. No, he was my Mr. Darcy that I had woken up to in 2016. He was the same to the very life. I rushed to my mother and waited for the Bingley company to come around the room and be introduced to us. All we had to do was look at each other and that would be all the introduction that we needed.

Eventually Sir William Lucas brought the Bingley set around to us, and while Kitty and Lydia were dancing once more, the rest of us were prepared and met them.

Yet when Mr. Bingley introduced him to us I was prepared for a warm welcome when he saw me, and joy of knowing that he was not alone in this strange world. However, Fitzwilliam Darcy looked on me coldly, and as if we had never seen each other before.

It then occurred to me that we hadn't. The Mr. Darcy I knew just happened to look like his ancestor therefore, in the same way that Elizabeth of 2016 looked like the spitting image of me. He looked like him, but he wasn't him. It hurt therefore, but just in case, I had to attempt one more thing, however foolish it would have me look.

As I curtsied to him, I smiled and whispered just loud enough for him to hear.

"Hobbit."

He looked at me with confusion.

"I beg your pardon, what did you utter?"

"Oh forgive me," I rushed out. "I merely had forgotten something and I was reminding myself of it, thank you."

Mr. Darcy (and I could not call this man Fitzwilliam) scowled at this and then looked away as my mother spoke to Mr. Bingley.

He truly wasn't my Mr. Darcy, and it set me backwards in my hopes, where I had felt dashed against the rocky shores of disappointment. For one moment, one fleeting moment, I thought that I had found him again. But I did not in the slightest.

And then I recalled something; a conversation that I had in London, while living with Fitz and his disgusting choice of a wife. I had promised him that I would look after his ancestor, for something tragic would befall him. If I could not have the one, at least I could keep my promise and help the other.

That was the last thing I had left to offer me hope and strengthen my purpose.

Therefore, out of admiration and love for the Fitzwilliam Darcy that I had lost, I would try and be there for this one. I looked at him once more as he stood there stiffly, looking about the room with a stone-like expression, it was my duty to try.

Therefore, it was time. Time to start all over again.

I accosted Mr. Darcy, and here is where it would all begin.

## End of Book I

Don't miss out on your next favorite book!

Join the Satin Romance mailing list
www.satinromance.com/mail.html

Dear Reader,

I hope that you enjoyed this time travel tale of Elizabeth Bennet and Mr. Fitzwilliam Darcy. I had never thought to do a time travel tale of this couple, for with my previous outings in P&P fanfiction, I only ever dabbled in time travel a couple years ago with the character Caroline Bingley in my other novel 'Girl Reaches Mars'/'I Dream of a Romance', but never the two central characters of Elizabeth and Fitzwilliam Darcy. I confess, that when I finally got up the nerve to do this, I had quite a great deal of fun when writing it.

Yet as I finished it, I realized that it did lend itself toward sequels if the audience liked the first one. Therefore, if you liked this book, and there are enough positive remarks on it where people enjoyed the story and wish to read further, then I shall do everything in my power to come up with an idea for a sequel. And I am certain I can come up with something. Yet if it is not well received, then you can't knock a girl for trying a new style, and thanks for picking it up anyway.

Sorry if I am going about this in a strange way, but I am a little green on figuring this sort of stuff out, for my audience has grown quite recently over my last few publications in ways that I did not foresee. Again, I hope you enjoyed it.

Ney Mitch

# THANK YOU FOR READING

Did you enjoy this book?

We invite you to leave a review at your favorite book site, such as Goodreads, Amazon, Barnes & Noble, etc.

## DID YOU KNOW THAT LEAVING A REVIEW...

- Helps other readers find books they may enjoy.
- Gives you a chance to let your voice be heard.
- Gives authors recognition for their hard work.
- Doesn't have to be long. A sentence or two about why you liked the book will do.

# About the Author

**Ney Mitch** has been a long-standing Jane Austen enthusiast, having written forty novels that were inspired by her various works. Since stumbling on Miss Austen's books after graduating from college, she has always dabbled in Austen inspired literature, ranging from writing works for teens to adults. Originally, her desire was to adapt Jane Austen's writing in a way to help young adults connect with her, however over time, she has spread her aims to other genres and styles.

Having received her BA Degree at Desales University, she is a writer, both literary and dramatic, as well as being a Historic Reenactor.

facebook.com/courtney.mitchell.589

twitter.com/CMMitchelPsyche

pinterest.com/shebaanna

# Also by Ney Mitch

Rapture & Rebellion

www.ingramcontent.com/pod-product-compliance
Lightning Source LLC
Chambersburg PA
CBHW050520260626
47157CB00004B/1402